Dear Gregory

You are my new friend "2 Die 4"

Enjoy

Maria

8/25/09

A Murder 2 Die 4

Marcia Slow-Sandler

authorHOUSE®

AuthorHouse™
1663 Liberty Drive
Bloomington, IN 47403
www.authorhouse.com
Phone: 1-800-839-8640

This book is a work of fiction. Names, characters, places, and incidents are the product of the author's imagination or are used fictitiously. Any resemblance to actual events, locales or persons, living or dead is entirely coincidental.

© 2009 Marcia Slow-Sandler. All rights reserved.

First published by AuthorHouse 7/27/2009

ISBN: 978-1-4389-8989-1 (sc)

Library of Congress Control Number: 2009905667

Printed in the United States of America
Bloomington, Indiana

This book is printed on acid-free paper.

For my Herb

*"I don't know exactly when dear,
But I'm sure we'll meet again dear.
And my darling till we do,
You Are Always In My Heart"*

Words and music by Kim Gannon & Ernesto Lecuona

with love and thanks

to my family

Eric, Michelle, Nicole, Howard and Lori

and with appreciation

for your help and support to

Irene (Renee) Staskin

Catherine (Cathy) Mavrak

Matthew (Matt) Banzin

Hallandale Beach Police Department
active and retired officers

Mardi Gras Gaming

to my friends

who gave me the encouragement to follow my dream.

I couldn't have done it without you

Chapter One

Thursday, January 31st

Thursday arrived cool, clear and bright. This kind of Florida morning was a cherished memory when the hot, steamy days of summer arrive.

Homicide detectives Manny Lopez and Cindy Anderson were deep into their morning briefing, reviewing the weekend arrest sheets when Officer Ken Richardson interrupted them.

"Road Patrol just called in a signal 7. A white female was found on the beach at US 1 and Sunset Beach Boulevard. Looks as though the cause of death is a broken neck. Officers Baker and Angel are on the scene."

Grabbing their radios, Lopez and Anderson hurriedly left the squad room. As their unmarked police car headed east toward the scene, the streets were still fairly quiet compared to the commuter traffic roaring along on I-95 just a mile to the west.

Sunset Beach is a bedroom community whose residents usually start stirring around nine a.m. Crimes here are mostly scams on the resurfacing of driveways, repairing roofs that didn't need to be repaired or the occasional purse snatching. But good God, *not* a homicide.

Since it is the height of tourist season, the media will have a field day with this story, the officers silently thought. Chalk this up as a Chamber of Commerce nightmare. Arriving at the scene, they were met by Officer Angel.

"What do you have so far?" Officer Baker asked as he took out his pad.

Checking her notes Officer Angel began to read, "At six a.m. a Hollywood couple, Vera and Bob Eaton, found the body. Stating they usually take this same walk every morning, they were surprised to see someone sleeping under a blanket. The tide was starting to come in so Bob Eaton left the boardwalk and walked down on the beach. As he approached what he thought was a sleeping figure, he was surprised to find that it was a woman. From the odd look on her face and her lack of color he shouted to his wife to call the police."

"What time did you and your partners get here?" asked Lopez.

Checking her watch Officer Diane Angel replied, "We got to the scene at six twenty-five a.m., and found the victim lying under a pink blanket. A white female, between the ages of 65 and 70, about 130 pounds and approximately 5 foot 6 inches. So as not to disturb any evidence, we waited until our Crime Scene Unit arrived. It did look from the angle of her head that she died from a broken neck."

Manny Lopez continued, "Did you find any of the victims ID, Diane?"

Shaking her head she added, "No, the victim's handbag is missing, which could lead us to believe that this is a purse snatching gone bad. What screws up this theory is that her shoes are also missing."

"Okay, keep the onlookers back on the boardwalk. Talk to the crowd and see if anyone saw anything this morning. Maybe we'll get lucky and find somebody who was partying late." Manny, bewildered, turned to Diane Angel and asked, "You did say her shoes are missing, didn't you?"

"Yes, I sure did" Diane agreed.

Detective Lopez turns to the two officers saying with a sigh, "Alright, talk with the couple that found the body then check to see if any pictures have been taken that can be distributed to the officers on road patrol. Let's try to keep a low profile on this for as long as we can. Maybe we can uncover some information before 'you know what' hits the fan."

Officer Angel headed for the The Crime Scene Unit (CSU) where she found several head shots of the victim ready to be passed out. Baker, Lopez and Anderson split up to talk to the crowd that had gathered. The officers on road patrol began canvassing the immediate neighborhood.

After four hours of knocking on doors in what is known as 'condo canyon', officers were able to identify the victim as Mrs. Joan Simpson –a long time Sunset Beach resident living on the 1900 block of North Ocean Drive.

The Medical Examiner does not resemble what one would expect when first meeting her. Tina Lange is 5 foot 10 inches tall with long auburn hair and finely chiseled features. She was pacing back and forth behind her desk, impatient that she couldn't reach Police Chief Mac Thomas directly. After making a twelve forty-five a.m. appointment through Chief's secretary, DeeDee, she headed back to the autopsy room. Any visitor passing her in the hall could easily think they were passing a fashion model rather than the county ME. Tina graduated in the top 10 of her class at U of M Jackson Memorial Hospital Medical School and went into the field of forensic medicine because she loved solving mysteries. She knew her medical expertise could help in homicide investigations that normally would have gone unsolved. Like a jigsaw puzzle, she could put the pieces together. Her curiosity and determination helped to put several killers behind bars, and now she is sure she had discovered something that will disturb the Chief.

The more Tina examined the body of Joan Simpson and re-read the police reports, the more this feeling of déjà vu continued to gnaw at her. There had been two cases in Lee County, where she had previously worked, that had too many similarities: same sex, same age bracket, each wore scarves; their deaths were the results of broken necks, and their shoes and handbags were no where to be found. In addition to that, all the victims were found lying under a pink blanket.

Comparing the similarities, she thought coincidence is an understatement. This is definitely the work of a serial killer. She checked her watch thinking twelve forty-five a.m. couldn't come soon enough.

At twelve forty-five a.m., Chief Thomas was seated behind his mahogany desk which was completely covered with files of varying thickness. He was hunched over a file when Tina knocked on the door and entered. The Chief is a big man, 6 feet 4 inches, and weighing in around 200 pounds, but no one should let his size fool them. He is quick on his feet and all muscle. Of course, he has to work out daily to stay in shape, especially since he hit the big 50.

"What's going on, Tina?" Chief asked as she entered the room motioning her to sit down.

"The circumstances surrounding the victim that was found this morning on Sunset Beach are very suspicious." The

Chief nodded for her to go on. "Well, when I was working in Lee County Medical Examiner's Office last year, we had two unsolved homicides that match this MO. All the victims were female, middle to late sixties. No shoes or handbags were found at the scenes and the causes of death were all broken necks. Oh, yes, let's not forget that they were all wearing scarves and were discovered lying under a pink blanket."

Tina became more animated as she continued to fill in the Chief and began to discuss the possibilities of a serial killer on the loose. Chief, leaning back in his chair, began to get a sickening feeling in the pit of his stomach. Just the thought of a serial killer here in Sunset Beach is disconcerting but to have something like this played out in the local newspapers at the height of the tourist season is a nightmare.

"Tina," he said, "can you please call some of your buddies in Lee County? Let them know what has happened here and ask for their help. Any information they can share will be greatly appreciated. I'm going to work on putting a Task Force together and will set up a meeting in the conference room at five. That should give us enough time to compile our information and compare it to whatever information the Lee County Sheriff's Office can put together." Pushing himself away from his desk, he walked Tina to the door. He was glad that he didn't feel it necessary to remind her to keep a closed lid on this. Knowing that Tina has street smarts as well as good looks, he watched her stride down the hall.

Returning to his desk he knew what he had to do to put this Task Force together before five pm. He jotted down the names and phone numbers of those who needed to be contacted and began with Assistant Chief Jimmie Kirk. Kirk was at a conference in Miami; he was able to reach him on his cell. Giving him the Reader's Digest version of what had taken place, Kirk assured him that he would leave the conference immediately and should be back in Sunset Beach about three. Chief Thomas turned his attention to his secretary DeeDee as she entered his office.

After handing her the list of the calls that she should make, he knew his next call should be to the local FBI's Miami Office. Chief had to convince himself that the reason he is calling for the FBI's help with this homicide is that they have the resources and the sophisticated equipment needed for the cross-referencing and profiling of suspected serial killers. He knew that deep down this really was the excuse he has been waiting for so he could contact Agent Francine Bolton.

He and Agent Bolton met when they had taken some courses together at the FBI Academy in Quantico about ten years ago and had a brief affair. When the classes ended, so did the affair. He and Francine agreed that it wasn't worth damaging his marriage or their careers so they parted friends.

Answering the phone on the second ring, Francine could not believe that it was Mac after all these years. "To what do I owe this unexpected phone call?" Her low warm voice had the Chief shaking inside as he explained the situation in Sunset Beach and told her he needed her help. He was delighted when she agreed to meet him at four o'clock that afternoon.

The next call on his list was to the City Manager John Roth who had earned the reputation of being a cynical, overbearing, insensitive tyrant. He had been with the city for more than ten years and looked much older than his 56 years. Since it was the City Manager's responsibility to keep the Mayor and the City Commissioners informed on any unusual happenings taking place in their fair city, Mac would have to bring him up-to-date on the recent homicide and the possibility of a serial killer on the loose.

Reaching his secretary Demetrius, Chief set up a meeting for three pm. He knew that he would need the City Manager's help to keep a tight lid on the details of the crime. He also was aware that convincing him that all information regarding this homicide would be on a *need to know basis* was also going to be an impossible task. Unfortunately, he and some of the Commissioners love to see their names in print and their faces on TV. One can bet even money that someone will say the wrong thing and jeopardize the investigation. It was essential that he be firm and insisted that all information be handled only through the Police Department's Public Information Officer, the PIO. He was sure that this crime will certainly be the lead story on the evening news. Checking his watch and seeing that it is only one fifteen p.m., his head began to pound and his stomach started to growl. He knew that this was going to be a long and difficult day.

Officers Bob Baker and Diane Angel had been assigned to gather all the information they could about the victim, Joan Simpson. That meant ringing doorbells and interviewing her neighbors. Arriving at 1997 South Ocean Drive, they made a decision to canvass the eight story building together. They were sure that most of the senior residents would be reluctant to open their doors, let alone speak to a police officer. Even with Officer Angel making the initial contact, they were still greeted with "I really don't know anything about Mrs. Simpson" or "I'm too sick to open the door." After several unsuccessful attempts, the officers chose to change their plan of attack.

"Let's find the Condo Commander," suggested Officer Baker. "I'm sure we'll get better results there".

There is a 'Condo Commander' in every complex. This is the one person that sees all, hears all and happily tells all. Luckily, when Baker and Angel rang the door bell at Apartment 4B, Mrs. Violet Kingston, the self-appointed Floor Captain, answered quickly.

"Come in, come in. Please sit down. Is it true that you found Joan Simpson murdered? You know she lived right on this floor in 4D? Silly me, of course you do or you wouldn't be here," she said with a little excited laugh.

Officer Angel asked, "Can you tell us anything about your neighbor that might help us with this investigation?"

"Well, Joan Simpson was a widow and lived in apartment 4D for the last eight years. She moved from Brooklyn, New York, after her husband and only child were killed in a car accident. She told me she's 65, but she was, at least, 70. if she was a day. I know she had a new boyfriend. He seemed like a real gentleman, always bringing her flowers, candy or wine."

"Can you give us his description?" asked Officer Angel with an encouraging smile.

"Not really," she replied. "I didn't want to be nosy so I only had a quick glance at him through my peephole when he was knocking on her door. Not that I spend all my time looking out my door, but as Floor Captain it is my responsibility to check on my neighbors. He was tall, slim and very neatly dressed. Oh, and his shoes were always highly polished."

"Can you tell us anything else?" Officer Angel asked.

"Well," Violet Kingston continued, "I did overhear Joan talking with Gwen Johnson from 4C. She was telling Gwen that she'd met this fellow at a meeting called 'Senior and Single'. The group meets at the library on US 1 and Sunset Beach Boulevard every other Monday night. You really should talk with Gwen. They were very good friends. In fact Joan gave

Gwen a key to her apartment even though the condo suggests the Floor Captain have the spare key in case of an emergency," she said with a hint of annoyance in her voice.

Both officers thanked Mrs. Kingston for her help and walked down the hall to apartment 4C. It was now 2:10. After receiving no response to their ring, they left their card stating they will return about four.

Back in the squad car Baker asked, "Feel like getting some lunch?" Angel nodded yes as she radioed in a 1040.

After lunch they again attempted to contact Gwen Johnson. They both hoped she would be as forthcoming as Mrs. Kingston had been.

"Maybe it would be a good idea for you to ask the questions" suggested Baker. "Woman to woman seems to make them more at ease."

When they arrived, they found Gwen Johnson nervously waiting for them. After identifying themselves, Officer Angel began the questioning. "What can you tell us about your neighbor Joan Simpson? Do you know if she has any relatives? Did she have any male friends? Anything you can tell us will help us find her killer."

Gwen Johnson listened to Officer Angel and then politely turned her back to her and gave her full attention to Officer Baker, thereby blowing the theory that women feel more comfortable talking to other women.

"Well, Officer Baker, let me just say I know you've already spoken to with Violet Kingston. She was quick to tell me all about your visit. God, she's such a busybody. You have to take what she said to you with a grain of salt. She's what we call a *yenta*. Do you know what that means?"

Baker smiles and said, "Yes, I think it means *busy body*. Please go on, Mrs. Johnson."

"Well okay. I went with Joan to the 'Senior and Single Club'. Of course, I only went because Joan didn't want to go alone, but, the group wasn't for me. Anyway she met this fellow Dick or Rick or something like that. As you can tell I'm not very good at remembering names, but I do remember he was young – maybe late 30's or early 40's. He was average height, dark hair, and I have to admit, kind of cute. I thought he was a little rough around the edges but Joan said that he reminded her of her late son. You know, the one that died in the car accident."

Officer Baker said, "We really appreciate all your assistance, Mrs. Johnson. Please call us know if you think of anything else that might be helpful."

"Oh, but there's more. And please call me Gwen," gushed Mrs. Johnson. "The second man she met was more her age. He was in his 60's, very dashing and impeccably dressed. He was always bringing her little gifts. Once she passed a remark that he must have been in the military because his shoes were always highly polished. I think his name was Albert or Allan something. I remember though that he drives a luxury car and always took her to expensive restaurants." Pausing to catch her breath she continued, "Do you know that Joan has a sister in New Jersey? Her first name is Roz. Maybe we can find her last name in her address book. You know I have the key to her apartment."

"Fantastic," said Baker, "but please don't touch anything when we go in. It could be the crime scene and we wouldn't want to disturb any evidence. You know that we aren't going to be allowed to remove anything from her apartment without a search warrant, and as the saying goes *we can look but we can't touch*."

Smiling Gwen Johnson said, "I promise to be careful."

Upon entering apartment 4D, Officer Angel headed straight for the kitchen where most people usually have a phone. Gwen Johnson followed closely behind. Officer Baker on the other hand, began a visual search of the rest of the apartment.

In the kitchen, right next to the wall phone, Officer Angel found Joan Simpson's personal phone book. As she started to leaf through the book, Gwen Johnson stopped her when she reached the "F" as she spotted a name she recognized.

"Wait; there it is. It's Fields. Roz Fields."

Officer Angel wrote down the name, the address in Montville, New Jersey, and the phone number. Calling out to Officer Baker, she told him that she found the sister's information and was ready to head back to the squad room.

Officer Baker responded, "Before we leave, you need to take a look at what I've found."

In an adjoining room, Officer Baker pointed to pictures of the late Joan Simpson each with four different males.

"Do you recognize any of these gentlemen?" he asked Gwen Johnson. When she answered yes, both officers felt that for the first time since the investigation began they had a place to start.

Chief Thomas' meeting with the City Manager went as he expected. As usual, the City Manager attempted to take charge of the investigation. The Chief was having trouble keeping his cool. After taking control of the meeting he assured the CM that he would be kept informed. They then discuss the handling of the media and finally agreed that the Public Information Officer, Raychel Casper would handle all media requests.

As Chief Thomas closed the door behind him, he knew it would only be a matter of time before all hell broke loose and the serene four square mile sandy beach community would be inundated with media from all over the U.S.

Making his next call he reached Sheriff Dan Wagner of the Lee County Sheriff's Office. Mac related the details of the recent homicide in Sunset Beach.

Sheriff Wagner interrupted Chief and said, "Mac, this has an unusually familiar ring to it. Did you know that we have two unsolved homicides with almost exactly the same MO's? Is your victim missing her shoes and handbag?"

"Yes, to both questions," Chief Thomas responds. "Your former Medical Examiner Tina Lange filled me in about your open cases earlier today.

Do you know that she is now working here in Broward County? Anyway, because of her concern that we may have a serial killer in our midst, I've decided to set up a Task Force to help investigate our homicide. I am hoping to enlist your aid so we can avoid duplicating our efforts."

Sheriff Wagner told Mac, "I'm going to assign Nick Russo to join your Task Force. Nick is the lead detective handling our cases. I'll reach him in the next few minutes so he can arrive in Sunset Beach in plenty of time for your meeting. In the meantime, I'll begin making copies of our files pertaining to our two homicides so that he can bring them with him."

"Oh, before I forget," Mac, grateful for the offer of cooperation asked, "were your victims found lying under pink blankets?"

Answering in the affirmative, Sheriff Wagner wishes him good luck and arranged to speak with Chief Thomas the following day.

FBI Agent Francine Bolton arrived exactly at three pm. Chief Thomas remembered what a stickler she was for punctuality as he waited for her at his office door.

"It's been awhile, Francine," he said. "You're still lookin' good."

With a sly smile and a quick kiss on the cheek, Francine replies, "You're not half bad yourself!"

Although it had been years since they have seen each other, Francine began to feel the chemistry between them returning. Trying to keep their relationship on a strictly professional basis was to prove harder than she had anticipated.

Mac tried to avoid small talk and immediately began to bring her up to date on the Joan Simpson case and what he had learned about the two unsolved Lee County homicides. They both came to the conclusion that to combine the resources of the FBI, Lee County Sheriff Department and the Sunset Beach Police Department would be advantageous to them all.

"I want it known that the rules of the game are that all agencies will cooperate with each other and that the Sunset Beach Police Department will be the lead agency. And all information will be disseminated through us. If this is agreeable, I'll appoint you to the Task Force right now."

"Not a problem," Francine agreed in her most professional tone.

"Okay, now that that's settled, the Task Force is meeting at five." Before loosing his nerve he asked, "How about catching a bite after that?"

Francine nodded yes and gave him a smile that sent a wave of pleasure through his body.

"See you at five" she said and headed for the door.

Sitting alone in his office, Mac came to grips with the realization that even after all these years he has missed her. He thought he had grown out of this infatuation but seeing her again rekindled all those old feelings. "Oh my God," he thinks, "I must be going through a mid-life crisis."

Settling behind his desk he called home and receiving no answer left a message for his wife. "Sorry Hon, I won't be home for dinner. I have to work late. Tell you all about it when I see you. I will try to call you later." Starting to feel guilty he made a mental note to bring home her favorite coffee cake.

Tina Lange recognized Nick Russo as he entered the squad room.

"Hey, Nick, nice to see you again," she smiled and shook his hand.

"Glad you could make it. The conference room's just down the hall. Could you use a cup of coffee before we head in?"

Russo shook his head, "No, I'm good. The ride was an easy one. I've brought the files on our two cases, so we might as well get started."

Russo is a 5 foot-10 inch, 175 pound, 38 year old with dark brown eyes and jet-black hair. He was born in Brazil. He has that Latin smile that could melt the heart of an Eskimo. A ten year veteran of the Lee County Sheriff's Office, he has spent five of those years in the homicide unit and the last two as the lead Detective on Lee County's two unsolved homicides.

The Task Force members were all settling in when Tina introduced Nick to them. Shaking hands with Chief Thomas and Sgt. Chris Burns, Nick nodded hello to Detective Manny Lopez and Officer Ken Richardson. After pulling out a chair for Tina, he took the vacant seat next to her. Placing the expandable file that he brought with him on the table, he is pleased that his department made enough copies for everyone on the Task Force.

Chief Thomas stood at the head of the table with a grim look on his face. "Detective Russo is here because of the two homicides in Lee County that have the same MO as ours. He's brought us the files from those cases." Nick began to pass them out. After asking everyone to take a few minutes to read the files, Chief saw Tina making notations on the forensic evidence starting with the cause of death, the broken neck. The other Task Force members were also listing questions, noting the similarities.

Detective Manny Lopez spoke first. Turning to Nick, Manny said, "Both your cases indicate the victims were missing their handbags and their shoes. Did you ever locate them?"

"No," Nick answers, "We couldn't find anyone who could remember what type of shoes they might have been wearing or what shoes are missing from the victims' wardrobes. Same with the handbags."

"What about the blanket?" inquires Sgt. Burns. "Our victim was found under a pink one. What about yours?"

"Yeah, so was ours. We can check your blanket against ours, but I don't think it will give you much to go on. Both of ours are common blankets that can be bought at any K-Mart, Wal-Mart or Flea Market." Officer Richardson stood up and stretched. The Task Force was in its second hour and all they had were even more unanswered questions.

Officer Richardson suggested that they put all the evidence in a secured locker, start fresh tomorrow, and only the authorized officers of the Task Force and the FBI's Forensic Unit could have access to it until the next meeting.

Agreeing with the suggestion, the Chief then turned to Tina and said, "I want you to be responsible for coordinating all the forensic information from Detective Russo and the Lee County Sheriff's Office. Check with the other ME's and see if they might remember anything that you can match to your findings."

Facing the group and in an unforgiving tone Chief said, "Listen up. I still have one more thing to say before you leave."

Getting their attention he continued, "Under no circumstances do I want to see or hear anything about this homicide in the papers or on TV. Do you all understand? The next of kin still hasn't been contacted. The only person permitted to talk to the press will be Raychel Casper, the PIO. There will be no exceptions. I can promise you that if there is any leak from this office, someone will be looking for a job. Any questions?" Receiving no response he said, "Good, the last thing we need is to scare the community with the threat of a serial killer lurking around."

The time was seven o'clock and the next meeting was set for four the following afternoon.

As Francine started to leave, Chief asked, "Francine, may I see you for a moment? I need some additional information from you regarding the availability of the bureau's computers"

Meeting Mac's eyes she answered, "Certainly."

When everyone had left the room, Mac took Francine's hand and asked her where she would like to have a bite. As she felt his touch, she tried to maintain her composure and asked in a low voice, "Shouldn't you be heading home?"

"No" Mac replied. "I left a message letting my wife know that I will be working late. Francine, I've really missed you. Can we go someplace where we can be alone and talk?" Wanting to take her in his arms, he stepped back knowing that this was simply not the place. As he looked into her eyes, he saw the twinkle he remembered and hoped that he was reading her correctly.

"Why don't you follow me back to my place, Mac? At least we won't have to worry about someone recognizing us." There is urgency in her voice, and as she touched his hand, they both felt the energy between them.

Her house is in the Miami Country Club development and both of them were delighted that it was only less than ten minutes away. After they entered her house, without uttering a word, Mac pulled her close and kissed her gently. This definitely is not a kiss of friendship, for after only a few seconds his tongue sought hers hungrily. Francine let out a soft moan of wanting. Her hands rose slowly to the back of his neck. As she stroked him ever so lightly, he felt his body shudder against her. Pulling back to look at her face, their eyes locked. As she dropped her jacket, he started to open the buttons on her blouse. There was no time to find the bedroom and no stopping them. Never releasing each other, they made passionate love on the couch. After a while Francine lead Mac to her bed where she began to make love to him again. He could not believe she could bring him back so quickly. Lying in each others arms, they felt like young lovers.

After a while Francine gently slides out of bed, puts on a robe and said, "Let me make us something to eat."

As she headed for the kitchen, Mac began to slowly dress and reminisced about what had just occurred. As he entered the kitchen he found Francine preparing an omelet. Looking up she suggested that they can either share a bottle of wine that is chilling in the refrigerator or find the scotch that is in the living room bar. Choosing the scotch, Mac headed for the living room and returned with a bottle of Glenfiddich.

Mac looked at Francine and asked, "Where do you think this relationship is heading?"

"Mac," she said, "we are going to have a drink, eat this wonderful omelet, then you will leave and go home. When we see each other tomorrow, we will be the professional police officers we have been trained to be." Feeling a surge of relief, Mac replied, "I guess that's the way it has to be." They clicked their glasses and tried to control their emotions. To mask the tears that started to pool in her eyes, Francine began to chop the onions.

After the Task Force group meeting ended, they all headed for the parking lot. "See you guys in the morning," Tina said with a wave of her hand. She was exhausted and very hungry. She turned to Nick who was walking along side her and asked, "Did you have time to find a place to stay?"

"No, I came right to the station. I hope I can find a place to crash since it is the height of the tourist season."

"Check out The Beach Inn," Tina volunteered. "It's reasonably priced and they always try to accommodate our out-of-town counterparts. It's right on Sunset Beach Boulevard and US 1. Don't forget to tell them you're here at Chief Thomas's request."

"Thanks. How about joining me for something to eat? I'm starving. Bet you are, too."

"Sounds inviting, but I'd rather head home, take a hot shower and order a pizza. But, if after you check in to your motel you find that you still have some energy, why not come over to my place and we'll share a pizza? I'm only ten minutes away."

Nick thought a moment and said, "Sounds good to me. Give me your number and I'll call for directions."

After registering at The Beach Inn, Nick drove around to his room. He threw his luggage on the bed and called home. He wanted to let his wife Joyce know where he was staying and bring her up to date on his schedule. She really hates it when he has to go out of town. Working late is one thing, but going out of town means that their twins are totally her responsibility; and they are a handful.

A Murder 2 Die 4

She answered on the third ring and sounded slightly out of breath. He then asked, "Is everything is okay?"

He and Joyce met in high school. It was the typical boy meets girl next door, boy marries girl, has two children and live happily ever after story. Well, at least, we got the children part right.

"I'm in the middle of giving the kids their bath," said Joyce, "and you know how agitated they get when you're not here to tuck them in."

He smiled. The twins were definitely living up to their names, Bonnie and Clyde. Whoever said cops didn't have a sense of humor didn't know Joyce and him. Some days he wondered if their house will still be in one piece when he finished his shift. A handful yes, but they are the loves of his life. What would he ever do without them? They make coming home each day tolerable. As six-year-olds, they are in perpetual motion and sometimes they required the patience of a saint just to get through the day. And for sure, Joyce is no saint.

Nick gave Joyce a little background on the Task Force and then gave her the Beach Inn's phone number but told her that he would keep his cell on when he wasn't in his room.

"Have you eaten?" Joyce inquires.

"No, not yet," he answers, "but I'm having a pizza with the ME. Have a good night and kiss the twins for me. I'll give you a call sometime tomorrow."

As Nick got into his car he thought about the fact that he had deliberately omitted the part that the ME is Tina Lange. Joyce might just remember having met her at a police social function and Joyce can blow any incident out of proportion. The fact that Tina is a stunning, unattached female did not influence his decision. Smiling he said to himself, yeah right. Why cause a fight over a fling that might never happen?

As he headed north he spotted a liquor store. Trying to decide between the red or white he grinned. Did it really matter which went with pizza? Grabbing a bottle of Chianti he continued on his way.

By the time Nick arrived at Tina's apartment she had showered, washed her hair slipped into her favorite CK jeans and ordered the pizza. While tying back her hair the doorbell chimed and she headed to the door.

As he entered, Nick handed Tina the wine saying, "This is for you for taking pity on an out-of-town colleague who hates to eat alone."

Tina showed Nick the apartment then pointed to the terrace she suggested that they eat outside and enjoy her incredible view.

Nick, leaning on the railing, breathed in the salty air. The evening was clear and a balmy 76 degrees with a full moon glistening over a pitch black, rolling ocean.

He thought that this is what people love about Florida.

Tina returned and passed Nick a goblet of Chianti and brought out the pizza that was delivered while Nick was admiring the view. Sitting at the table, they watched the full moon rise. They each took a slice of pizza covered with peppers, onions, olives, mushrooms, ground beef, three kinds of bubbling cheeses and pepperoni.

Smiling Tina said, "I can't stand having to make decisions when I leave the office, so I ordered the pizza with everything on it."

Laughing Nick said, "Great choice; the pizza is delicious."

Finishing the pizza they sat back, sipped the Chianti and discussed the homicides.

Tina sighed and said, "I can just see the headlines now: *Golden Girls'* Murderer Commits Number Three. With all the victims being female and over 65, the media will love comparing them to that 80's TV series about the four senior citizens living together in Miami".

Tina then headed for the kitchen to make coffee. "Stay there and relax" she said. "I'll bring the coffee out in a couple of minutes."

When she returned she found Nick fast asleep on the lounge chair. Some hot date he turned out to be, she muses. Might as well let him sleep the wine off. She returned with a blanket and covered Nick as he snored softly. She smiled when she realized that her blanket is pink. Well, that's a little spooky, she thought.

Returning to the living room, she turned on the late news and stretched out on the couch. Soon, like Nick, she was sound asleep.

Chapter Two

Friday, February 15th

Traffic on I-95 North was moving smoothly. The long, white moving van took the Sunset Beach exit and headed east to the beach. The driver spotted the "Welcome to Sunset Beach" sign and glanced at his watch. "Not bad," he thinks, "I missed the morning rush hour. Here it is six forty-five a.m., and I'm almost at the address. Should be an easy day." He looked in his side-view mirror to make sure his client was still behind him. The late model silver Jaguar, driven by a gentleman in his mid 60's, signaled to exit the interstate.

The van passed through several walled communities that make up the city known as Sunset Beach. He drove over the bridge, and turned South on US1. On his left was a sign that read "Welcome to the Towers Beach Condominium". The silver Jag pulled out and passed in front of the moving van. It stopped in front of the guard gate. The driver is a distinguished looking gentleman with a little gray appearing at his temples in his reddish-brown hair, revealing piercing blue eyes, and a rich tan. He wore an expensive looking silk striped sport shirt open at the neck, warm beige slacks with sharp edged pleats, and a navy blue cashmere blazer. He looked like someone who had just stepped from the pages of "GQ".

Allan Grimm greeted the security guard by wishing him a good morning and introduced himself as the new tenant in building 1250, apartment PH 10. The guard jotted down the license plate numbers of the car and van and asked Mr. Grimm to see some form of ID. After showing his drivers license, Allan Grimm received his tenant's pass from the security guard who proceeded to open the gate allowing the car and moving van to enter the complex. After finding a reserved space marked PH 10, Allan Grimm parked his car while the van backed up to the service entrance to building 1250. As the movers began to unload the van to start bringing its contents into the building, Allan Grimm stepped into the elevator and pressed PH. Whisked quietly yet quickly to the penthouse floor, the door opened revealing his front door opposite the elevator, just as he requested. He is pleased.

As he opened the door to his luxury apartment, he headed for the wrap around terrace. Stepping out he breathed in the cool morning air and whispered, with a faint smile on his tan face, "Here I go again."

As the moving men continued to unload the van, the four ladies sharing their morning coffee in their card room looked out the window and began to speculate on the new tenant.

"Is there a missus? Does he have children? What does he do for a living? Where is he from?" Each of the women present knew that if he turned out to be an eligible bachelor, he'd be quickly included on the social circuit.

Beth Landers, one of the four observers, said, "Just a minute. This must be the new tenant that rented the Levitans' apartment on my floor. Give me a little time and I'll see what I can find out about him." Getting up from the table she headed for her apartment. The remaining ladies continued to drink their coffee as they smiled knowingly. When Beth started a "new project" she wouldn't stop until she found out all they'd need to know about him.

While the moving was going on down the hall, Beth prepared a pitcher of iced tea and arranged some of her homemade chocolate chip cookies on a tray. Standing in her new neighbor's doorway, Beth could see him as he was waiting for the last piece of furniture to be put in place. Walking towards him, she greeted him, "Hi, I'm Beth Landers. Welcome to the building. I thought you might like to take a break about now and I have made some iced tea and cookies for you."

"Well, hello, Beth Landers. I'm Allan Grimm. How thoughtful of you! It certainly will hit the spot." Beth left and returned with the iced tea and cookies. Allan invited her in.

As she poured the iced tea, she looked around the apartment and at the furnishings Allan Grimm had brought with him and was impressed. After about ten minutes of chatting, Beth decided that she had all the information she needed to report back to her friends, at least for right now. She had learned that he is a retired children's clothing designer and has been a widower for the past two years. He has two daughters living in New York, and is a grandfather of four. Not bad for ten minutes of conversation, she grins.

"I know you must have a million things to do so let me leave you. You can return the tray later, no rush. I'm sure we'll be seeing a lot of each other since we'll be sharing the same elevator. Knock on the door if I can help you with anything."

Beth returned to her apartment and immediately called her three friends, telling each one that she has the 'scoop' on the new tenant and that she would meet them at the usual time and they'd eat at their usual place.

At precisely noon, the four ladies, who are referred to by their friends as "The Ladies That Lunch" (TLTL), were seated in their Club House, ordered lunch and began to discuss the latest topic: Allan Grimm. Beth proudly shared all the information she had acquired about him. After lunch she proposed that they head to the Aventura Mall for some serious shopping, but before she could finish her sentence, Pam reminds her that they have a crime watch meeting that afternoon at three regarding the COP program (Citizens On Patrol). Acknowledging that they remembered the meeting, they decided to order dessert instead.

The Crime Watch Board meeting held in the Sunset Beach Police Department building was just getting under way when Beth, Maxine, Pam and Judy arrive. Apologizing for being late, they took their seats. They were really excited about the new project that the City Commissioners had endorsed. Feeling like Cagney and Lacey, they couldn't wait to get started. They have decided that Beth and Judy would be one team and Maxine and Pam would be another. When informed that they will be issued cell phones, they felt very important. Even though they can only use them to dial either 9-1-1 or the Sunset Beach Police Department, it still made them feel special.

Gary Davis, the Police Liaison Officer to Crime Watch, welcomed the group and while handing out the course outline and copies of the Broward County Uniform Signals Codebook, thanked them for volunteering to help start this program. During the session, Officer Davis stressed the importance of the uniform codes. Explaining that some codes and signals are more crucial than others he instructed the class to memorize the ones that he had highlighted.

Moving on, he also stressed the fact that Crime Watch is the 'eyes and ears' of the police department and emphasized that they are not sworn officers. Their only responsibility is to 'observe and report' incidents and, under no circumstances, are they to become physically involved. After the presentation, Officer Davis conducted a question and answer period. When the session ended at four thirty p.m., TLTL called it a day and headed home.

Chapter Three

Saturday, February 2nd

As she stirred, Tina felt a vibration, and discovered that it was coming from the cell phone that Nick must have left on the couch. She yawned and stretched. "Oh my God," she realized as she came awake, "I must have slept here all night!" Slowly the evening came into focus. Hurriedly she headed for the terrace, found Nick sound asleep, shook him awake and handed him the phone. Groaning he tried to get off the lounge chair.

Turning to Tina, Nick said painfully, "I should have gone back to the motel. My back is going to kill me all day." Checking the number of the missed phone calls, he knew that he is in big trouble. It was Joyce trying to reach him.

"I'll make coffee while you check in." Tina moved towards the kitchen giving Nick some privacy.

He redialed the number and was greeted with, "Where the hell have you been, you bastard!" Joyce screamed. "While you're out sleeping around I had to take Clyde - you do remember your son, don't you? - to the emergency room. He fell down the stairs and broke his leg and they had to perform emergency surgery.

"How is he?" Nick started to ask but the line is already dead. He knew that it was a waste of time to try to reason with Joyce when she goes off the deep end like this, so he dialed Lee Memorial Hospital in Fort Myers and asked to be connected to the pediatric floor.

Introducing himself as Detective Nick Russo, he said, "I understand from my wife, that my son Clyde was operated on last night to repair his broken leg. How is he doing?"

"My name is Susan Stevenson, Detective Russo, and I've been assigned to your son. He's resting comfortably, and I'm sure he'll be able to come home in a few days. He's had a nasty break, but we don't expect any complications. I'm on till seven this evening so if you want to call later, I'll be glad to give you an update on his condition." Thanking her for her kindness and with relief in his voice Nick tells the nurse that he will call back before her shift ends.

Hanging up, he found Tina in the kitchen. She handed him a steaming mug of coffee. "Sorry about all this. My son was rushed to the emergency room last night and my wife was calling me. By the way, we're separated."

"You don't owe me an explanation," Tina said as she sipped her coffee.

"But I want to. Joyce and I have been having problems for a long time. We tried counseling but nothing seems to help. She has had mental problems for awhile and her suspicious nature has turned into a kind of paranoia. I spoke to her shrink and he thought it would be better for her treatment if we did a trial separation. Fortunately for Joyce, her parents have agreed to pay for 24/7 care for the children. Even so I'm still debating whether or not I should have left."

"Let me give you Chief Thomas' home number," Tina said. "Call him and explain about your son's accident. I'm sure he'll give you time off so you can drive home to see your son. He's really a great guy. The Task Force can move ahead, and I'll keep you up-to-date on a daily basis." After he thanked her, Tina handed him her phone.

Nick reached the Chief on the first ring and quickly apologized for the early morning call. He proceeded to explain his situation at home.

"Go ahead and take as much time as you need. We'll keep you in the loop," the Chief responded.

"I figure if I leave right away, I can be back for the four o'clock Task Force meting."

"That's not necessary, Nick, the Task Force will have notes that can be faxed to you up there. Take a couple of days off till your son gets back home. We have plenty to do on our own. Besides I want you to concentrate 100% on the homicides when you do get back here."

Nick thanked the Chief adding, "I'm heading home now. I'll stay overnight, and if everything is all right, I'll be back tomorrow. I'll call you and let you know when I'm leaving".

After hanging up, Chief Mac continued to shave while thinking about their conversation. He wondered why Nick was so insistent about getting back for the Task Force meeting. Hell, you'd think his son would be his first priority. Maybe he's just eager because the two unsolved homicides make him look bad. As the lead detective, the brass may have made him feel that he screwed up. He could be taking this case personally and that could be a problem. You don't think clearly when you take an investigation personally. I need a team player. Chief remembers, as a rookie, he had a Captain that told him to always trust your gut instinct. Well, his gut right was warning him to keep a close eye on Detective Nick Russo.

With his mind in overdrive even before the five-thirty am phone call, Chief had decided to get a head start on his paper work. He had an agenda item that was due before the Commission tomorrow and he hadn't even begun the back up paper work. Oh well, he thought, maybe I'll have a little peace and quiet before the daily interruptions start. Entering his office through the back door, he settled in front of his computer with his favorite breakfast: a large black coffee and a buttered bagel from Dunkin Donuts. As he took his first sip of the steaming hot coffee, he was surprised when his phone rang.

"Chief....," and before he can say Thomas, Phyllis, the dispatcher at the front desk, cut him off.

"Chief, it's Phyllis. What's going on? I've got the lobby jammed with radio and TV station reporters. They've packed the parking lot with their vans and equipment and our guys can't find spaces. These guys are insisting there's a serial killer loose in Sunset Beach and that they aren't leaving without a statement or a press release. I tried telling them that our PIO comes in at nine. They told me that they recognized your car as you drove in so they know you're in the building. What should I do?" Phyllis lowered her voice to a whisper, "Is it true? I mean about there being a serial killer on the loose?"

"Phyllis, it's on a need to know basis and believe me when I say, you don't need to know," the Chief replied. "The less you know," he continued, "the easier it will be for you to do your job. Just hold down the fort. When I'm ready to hold a major press conference, I promise you'll know exactly what's going on. Till then you're better off in the dark. You can honestly say, I don't know. Now call Raychel Casper and tell her I need her here ASAP. Call her at home and not on her cell. Tell her that the 'you know what' has hit the fan. Also tell her to use the back door and not to answer any questions if the media stops her. Oh hell, she knows the drill; just tell her to move it as fast as she can. Christ, now I've got to call Assistant Chief Kirk and alert the City Manager. Damn, I'll have somebody's badge for leaking this to the press if it's the last thing I do. Which Captain's on duty?"

"It's Captain Pollack on Alpha shift."

"Find him and tell him to call in the Task Force. I want them in my office in one hour. No excuses. Right now, we need damage control. If the media starts to give you a hard time, have the Captain escort them out of the building."

"But, Chief, it's raining" she interrupted.

"I don't give a damn. I won't allow them to disrupt my department. They know the rules and if they've forgotten them, well, we'll just remind them, rain or no rain."

As he hung up, he looked at his watch knowing it was going to be one hell of a day. He could feel the pounding in his temples and the knot in his stomach clenched a little tighter.

Just when he thought things couldn't get worse, Phyllis was back on the phone. "Sorry, Chief, I know this is really going to piss you off, but half the Crime Watch board just walked in and the press is heading right for them. What should I do?"

"Just put them in one of the conference rooms and tell them we'll be there shortly. Have you reached Raychel yet?"

Phyllis answered, "Yes, she should be here any minute."

"Okay, let me know when she gets here."

Hanging up the phone, Chief thought to himself that this is just what I don't need -- fucking civilians who think they're cops and expect to be kept informed. Yeah, right.

During this time, Nick was on the road heading on I-95 towards Alligator Alley, which connects east and west Florida. Traffic was light so Nick hit his home number on his cell.

"Hi, it's me. Before you start in on me, listen ...just listen. I told you I had to come down here because of a homicide. It turns out to have the same MO as those two other unsolved cases I'd been investigating in Lee County. The two women who were missing their shoes and handbags, remember? The same items are missing in this homicide on Sunset Beach. We're all thinking we might have a serial killer on the loose. I worked with the Task Force through the night. I never looked at my cell until we took a break. When I checked my phone I saw that my battery died." Pausing for effect, Nick continued, "One of the cops lent me a charger and when it powered up I saw our number and called you right away." Holding his breath Nick hoped that Joyce bought this story and would calm down.

Joyce promptly answered, "Nick, I'm so sorry I flew off the handle. I should have known there was a good reason for you not picking up. Please forgive me. I know I over-react when something happens to the one of the twins. Don't worry about Clyde. He's going to be fine". Trying to lighten the mood she reminded Nick that she is still a nurse. "I'll meet you at the hospital; just drive carefully." Sounding like the perfect wife and mother, Joyce hung up. Relieved that she bought his story, Nick began to think about Joyce's nursing career. Smirking, he thought, that's some joke. Joyce claimed that she was still a nurse. When she finally graduated and went to work she decided that working in a hospital was too intense and a doctor's office too dull. So that left her working at a local assisted living facility where the 'inmates', as she referred to them, drove her crazy with their incessant questions and constant demands. Getting pregnant was her way out and when she gave birth to the twins, they became her full time job. So much for her nursing career!

Pulling into the drive-thru at Burger King he ordered a large black coffee, then settled back in his seat, bracing himself for the long boring drive on Alligator Alley.

Once through the toll booth there was not much to do except to stay awake and drive. Nick tried to imagine what Joyce would do to him if she ever found out he'd spent the night in Tina's apartment. No way could he convince her that he fell asleep on the terrace and that nothing happened.

Thinking back he remembered that Joyce took an instant dislike to Tina the one time that she met her at the Police Benevolent Association fundraiser. When he asked her about her animosity towards a woman she just met, Joyce responded with something about disliking red heads. That's part of Joyce's problem. You never know how she'll react. There is never a logical answer to anything she said or does. "God, I hope she never finds out," Nick muttered to himself. "Why do I stay with her? The answer is simple there are two compelling reasons. The first is Bonnie and the second is Clyde."

Finally reaching the hospital, he was grateful that it only took two hours including the stop at the drive thru. Looking for a parking space, Nick spotted Joyce talking on her cell phone near the front entrance to Lee Memorial Hospital. He beeped the horn and as he turned into a parking spot saw Joyce quickly put her phone away.

"Hey, Good Looking," Joyce said as she approached Nick. "You're right on time."

Nick kissed Joyce on the cheek as he stepped out of the car. "How's Clyde doing?"

"He's doing fine, now." Hooking her arm through Nick's, they entered the lobby and Joyce suggested they pick up some stuff for Clyde. After gathering up balloons and comic books, Nick and Joyce headed for the 3rd floor Pediatric section.

As the elevator door slid open, Nick spotted Clyde lying in a room that looked as though Walt Disney himself had decorated it. If one had to be sick and a kid again this is the place to be. He leaned over to kiss Clyde on the forehead and said, "Hey big guy, how are you feeling?"

"Daddy, Daddy. You came home," squeals Clyde as Nick tied the balloons to his night table.

"Of course I'm here. You know that nothing could keep me away. When Mommy called and told me you were in the hospital, I left Sunset Beach right away. That was a pretty bad fall you had." Clyde nodded his head vigorously. Continuing Nick asked, "How did it happen? Were you playing at the top of the stairs?" Before he could ask another question, Clyde leaned over and whispered so that Joyce could not hear and confided to Nick, "I'm not allowed to talk about it cause if I do, I'll be in real trouble." Not wanting to cause his son any more stress, he decided to drop the subject, but vowed to get to the bottom of this. Just then a nurse entered the room.

"Good morning, Joyce," the nurse said while turning away from Nick, "your parents just called to say they will be here this afternoon."

"Thanks for taking the message. By the way, this is my husband, Nick."

"Yes, I can see the resemblance to Clyde. Nice of you to come home to your family" the nurse said with a cold stare. With that she left the room.

Nick could only imagine how Joyce had described him to anyone who would listen. He has been through this before. Joyce has a knack of gaining sympathy from strangers especially when she gives only her side of a story. Then he finds that he has to spend time defending himself to people he doesn't know or for that matter care about. "Hell, I don't have time for this shit. She just better pay attention to Clyde," he muttered to himself.

By ten am, Nick had finished reading several comics to Clyde, helped him eat some of his breakfast and spoke with the doctors. Turning to Joyce, he said, "I'm going to head back to the house so I can call Chief Thomas and spend some time with Bonnie before I have to head back to Sunset Beach."

Clyde looked up from his comic. "Daddy, will you come back to see me?" his eyes filled with tears. "Mommy brought maps with directions to Sunset Beach so we can see where you're staying. Can Bonnie and I come visit you there?"

"Oh, Clyde, don't you worry. I'm not going to live in Sunset Beach. I'm only working there temporarily. I'll be home before you know it. I'm never going to move away from you and Bonnie. You know that I love you both. You know we both have jobs. My job is to catch the 'bad guys' and your job is to concentrate on getting better. Grams and Poppie will be here soon so why don't you try and take a nap until they come?" Nick gave Clyde a big smile and kissed him good bye.

Joyce asked if everything was okay. Nodding yes, Nick wondered why Joyce would have gotten a map to Sunset Beach.

After leaving the hospital in separate cars, Nick stopped at his apartment to pick up the mail.

Joyce arrived at the house slightly ahead of Nick so he parked his car behind hers. As Joyce got out and opened the front door, an animated little girl ran out shouting, "Daddy!

Daddy!" and jumped into his arms even before he was able to close his car door.

Cradling her and holding her tightly, he asked, "Did you miss me?" He hugged and kissed Bonnie. Realizing that she is shivering in his arms, he asked, "What's the matter, baby? Are you cold?" and hugged her even tighter. With her arms around his neck, squeezing him as hard as her small arms could, she whispered, "I'm not cold, Daddy, I'm scared. I'm so glad you came home. All Mommy does is scream. She even screams at Grams and Poppie. Why is she always so mad?" Continuing to ramble, she asked, "and why is she so mad at you? What did you do wrong? Didn't you listen to her? Are you in big trouble?" Bewildered, Nick tried to reassure her that everything is all right. Still shaking, Bonnie said, "Daddy, Mommy really scares me sometimes." Tilting her head to one side as children do, she looked into his eyes and asked, "Why don't you sleep here any more? Mommy told me and Clyde that it was our fault because we're bad and don't listen to her." Finally running out of breath, Bonnie whimpered, "We promise we'll be good. Please, Daddy, please come home." Nick kneeled to calm down and tried to hold himself in check. He resisted the urge to grab Joyce by the throat and rip her fuckin' heart out. He carried Bonnie into the house telling her that Mommy didn't mean those things she said and it isn't their fault. They didn't do anything wrong. Mommy is just very upset about Clyde's accident and that everything will be better as soon as he comes home from the hospital." Knowing that he will have to get to the bottom of this, he decided to call his in-laws as soon as he can get some privacy. He has made up his mind that he was not going to leave until the problem with the children is settled.

Continuing to calm Bonnie down, he asked, "How about we order a pizza for lunch and you can show me what you've been doing in school?"

"OK," she agreed as she pulled Nick into the house.

After ordering pizza Nick asked Joyce, "Okay if I use the phone to call Chief Thomas?" Joyce nodded yes.

Reaching Chief, Nick explained, "It's taken me a little longer than I planned so I won't make the five o'clock Task Force meeting. Clyde's doing okay and should be home in a few days. I will be getting back to Sunset Beach tonight and was hoping it would it be possible for me to meet you after the meeting, maybe over dinner, so you can bring me up to date?"

"Alright" said Chief. "I have an eight o'clock meeting tonight with the vice-president of Mardi Gras Gaming, Dan Adkins, regarding a donation for the PAL softball league. Meet me there and I'll introduce you to him. Adkins is a great guy, and is always the first one to come through whenever we need help for any children's project. Food's pretty good and besides the slots and poker, the dogs are running. I'll see you in the third floor restaurant anytime after eight."

As he hangs up Nick thought a good dinner, watching a few races and playing slots, are not a bad way to spend an evening. Nick, hearing the front doorbell left the room to meet the pizza delivery man and noticed Joyce standing in the doorway of their bedroom.

Having listened to his conversation she turned away and thought at least he'll have dinner with the Chief and not some tramp he's picked up in Sunset Beach.

The Ladies That Lunch (TLTL) met at the Clubhouse to discuss the new tenant Allan Grimm. They decided that it is time for a reintroduction. They convinced Beth to return to the building and instead of going straight to her apartment, she should visit Allan Grimm using the ruse that she needed to reclaim her cookie tray and iced tea pitcher.

Taking a deep breath, Beth knocked on his door and heard, "Just a second, I'll be right there." After a minute or two the dead bolt lock opened and Allan Grimm, dressed in black slacks with a cream colored Geoffrey Bean golf shirt, opened the door.

"Beth, what a pleasant surprise. Come on in. I'm sorry to keep you waiting but I was out on the terrace enjoying the view and decided to polish my shoes while I was out there."

"Well, I can't stay but a minute," responded Beth. "I came to ask if my cookie tray and pitcher are available."

"Of course they are. I should have returned them to you," and as he apologized, he headed into the kitchen. returning quickly with the tray and pitcher.

"How's the settling in going?' inquired Beth.

"Fine, but you know it's always hard moving into a new neighborhood. You haven't gotten to know your neighbors as yet so it's lonely in the beginning." Flashing a Colgate Smile, he added, "At least I've had the pleasure of meeting you." Then pausing only a moment, he asked, "Would you like to join me for dinner tonight? That is, if you don't mind the short notice. I'll understand if you already have plans."

Demurely she answered, "Yes, that would be nice."

Allan reminded her that he is new in town and asked if she has a restaurant of which she particularly fond. Thinking for a moment, Beth suggested a new restaurant that had just opened in Hollywood. She told him that she had been dying to try it. "It's called *The Fabulous Fishery*." Then blushing she added, "I should have asked if you like seafood."

"My problem is I like all food" he answered with a smirk on his face. "I'll make a reservation for seven o'clock if that's all right with you?"

"That's fine," said Beth as she turned toward the door. "I'll see you then around six-thirty."

Walking to her apartment Beth felt giddy with excitement. She couldn't wait to call the girls and give them the news, but knowing that she needed to get her priorities in order, her first call went to her hairdresser. Making a one-thirty appointment, her next call was to Judy. Judy is one of TLTL to whom Beth felt the closest. Judy was ecstatic to hear about Beth's date and offered to let the rest of the girls know so that Beth could be on time for her beauty parlor appointment. She told Beth that she'd make the arrangements for them to all meet at the Clubhouse the next day and teasingly told her that they'll want all the details.

"Hey, maybe I should take notes so I don't leave anything out" Beth said jokingly before hanging up.

Arriving at the hairdresser, Beth saw the receptionist and the manicurist huddled around the TV set. "What's up?" Beth questioned.

The receptionist replied, "Where have you been all morning"? Haven't you heard the latest news? It's all the stations are reporting. The police found the body of an older woman on the beach. They haven't released her name as yet. Something about the next of kin, but the press has started calling it the Golden Girls Murder."

"I hope it's no one we know," Beth replied. "I've haven't listened to the news this morning and I don't want to hear anything that's depressing. I refuse to allow anything to spoil my day. So let's change the subject please."

Arriving home at three-thirty Beth went straight to her closet to look for the right outfit to go with the new upsweep. She felt young, again and settled on the navy dress she wore to Judy's 65th birthday party. Beth knew her legs were still in good shape and the dress just skimmed her knees showing off her tennis calves and trim ankles. She pulled out her Steve Madden navy and white Spectator pumps and the navy Prada handbag her daughter had given her. Running a bubble bath she positioned her neck pillow and eye mask and then sank into her tub.

At exactly six-thirty, her doorbell rang. There stood Allan Grimm with the most exquisite bouquet of flowers she had ever seen.

"Did you run into much traffic on the way over?" she asked smiling.

"Funny you should ask. It was bumper to bumper people," he said laughing. She carried her flowers into her kitchen and searched for a vase that would do them justice.

"That is a beautiful outfit," Allan said admiringly. "Your shoes and handbag are the perfect finishing touches. I love going out with a woman who enjoys dressing up for dinner. And I like your new hairstyle. It's very becoming." Beth just blushed.

When they entered the restaurant, the TV in the bar area was tuned to the local news with anchor Steve Weston reporting the victim to be Joan Simpson, a 65 years old widow, living alone in a condo in the 1900 block of South Ocean Drive. Her next of kin had been notified. Beep, beep, beep, the TV sounding the alert warning as the news bulletin flashes across the bottom of the screen reported.

...We have just confirmed a report that two similar homicides have taken place in Lee County. The Sunset Beach

Police Department and Crime Stoppers asks that if you or someone you know has any information that could shed any light on this latest murder, please contact them. The phone numbers are on display at the bottom of the screen.

Even though they were seated, Allan was still watching the news report. He then turned his to attention Beth as soon as the station returned to its regularly scheduled program and asked, "What would you like to order?"

Scanning the extensive menu Beth thought about how nice it was to go out to dinner without ordering from the dreaded early bird menu. Beth chose the crispy salmon steak; Allan chose the red snapper; and they agreed to share a Caesar salad. Ordering a bottle of Pinot Grigio they settled back in their chairs and began to chat. Beth found Allan an easy person to talk with although he was not too open about himself. He did tell her he lived on Sanibel Island for about six months before coming to Sunset Beach. He was also a good listener as she told him a little about herself. By the time they finished dinner and reached their condo, Beth and Allan sounded like two long time friends. Riding the elevator together to the Penthouse floor, Beth secretly hoped Allan would ask her out again.

As they reached her door she extended her hand and said, "Allan, I'm so glad you asked me to dinner. I don't remember the last time I had such a pleasant evening."

Allan took her hand gently to pull her toward him and kissed her on the cheek. "It was my pleasure. I too, had a wonderful evening. It's been quite awhile since I dined with a woman who is as attractive and charming as you. I hope you'll consider this the beginning of a long-term friendship. Would you care to have dinner with me again this Sunday?"

Beth seemed almost shy as she accepted his invitation.

After locking the door behind her Beth kicked off her shoes and waltzed around her living room. As she undressed and stepped into her nightgown she found herself hoping that this acquaintance could turn into something more then a casual relationship. As Beth put a glass of water on her night table she saw her answering machine blinking. The display window showed that there were three messages. Knowing without even playing them back, they were from Pam, Maxine and Judy. "They just can't wait to hear about my evening. Well, I think I'll keep them in suspense until tomorrow." She turned on the eleven o'clock news and shut off her light.

At four-thirty Chief's secretary DeeDee prepared the second floor conference room for the second Task Force meeting. Thinking about setting a place for herself she decided that it's the best way to get all the information first hand. DeeDee has worked for the Sunset Beach Police Department for 23 years and though she talks about retiring, something always comes up to make her put those plans on hold.

DeeDee is an elegant looking lady. Tall, blonde and soft-spoken. Meeting her for the first time you might describe her as almost angelic. But those who know her on a personal level know better. DeeDee was really a tough cookie and could get down in the dirt with the best of them. You didn't want to tick her off; it was better have her as a friend than to have her as an enemy. Pushing sixty-three, she has developed a keen instinct for sizing people up. Her first impressions are uncanny. Through the years the department would often ask her to sit in on interviews and her evaluations were right on the money. It was hard to remember the last time DeeDee was wrong.

Turning as she heard footsteps, DeeDee acknowledged Detective Manny Lopez's arrival.

A Murder 2 Die 4

"Take any spot you want" she said.

Detective Lopez could be easily described as a character. An ex-New York cop, his thick Brooklyn accent was his trademark as well as part of his charm. Manny's been with the department for twelve years with eight of them in the Detective Bureau. His expertise is in the details. He is fanatic about the little things and drives the others in the unit crazy. Manny has the ability of finding evidence that others think is insignificant. His nickname is 'Columbo' and like his T.V. counterpart, he drives an old beat up car, smokes smelly cigars and always looks as though he's slept in his clothes. He even wears a wrinkled raincoat. The question around the department is did they pattern Columbo after Manny or did Manny copy Columbo? Anyway, don't ever sell him short.

While pulling out a chair, Manny asked DeeDee, "When you're done setting up the room will you make copies of my notes? I want to grab a cup of coffee and I need to distribute these to the team."

"No," DeeDee said, "get off your butt and do it yourself. You pass the fuckin' copier before you get to the coffee room. I may be a secretary, but I'm sure as hell not yours!"

Manny, pissed, kicked the chair backwards and headed out the door giving DeeDee a dirty look while muttering under his breath. With an amused smile on her face, DeeDee can make out only one word -- *bitch*.

Sgt. Chris Burns was the next to arrive. Having made sergeant just one month earlier, he is still not comfortable in his new position or being on the Task Force. He's nice looking, about 35, and was recently married. His expertise is in fingerprint identification. Even though the department is fully computerized, certain details still need to be categorized the old fashioned way.

Tina arrived with her arms loaded with files. "Hey, Chris how's our new sergeant?" she asked as she dropped the files on the table.

"Hanging in there, I guess," he said.

"I'm heading for some food. Can I get you something?' Tina inquired. She had spent the entire morning on the phone with the M.E.'s offices from Lee, Monroe and Palm Beach counties. Between phone calls, faxes and making copies she realized that she hadn't eaten lunch.

"Nah, I'm good," Burns answered.

Tina grabbed chocolate chip cookies, peanut butter crackers and a diet coke, and headed back to the conference room.

While waiting for Tina to take her seat, Chief Thomas re-introduced Special Agent Francine Bolton to the Task Force. As he started to outline Francine's involvement with the case, DeeDee raised her hand and interrupted him.

"Chief, why do you feel the need to involve another agency in our investigation?"

Looking annoyed, he answered, "I know you all are concerned about the FBI taking over the case, but with Francine on board we can minimize that from happening."

DeeDee interrupted once again, voicing what everyone else was thinking but didn't have the guts to say aloud, "It's our case. Why do we want an outside agency horning in on our investigation and stealing the limelight?"

Before anyone else could voice his or her displeasure, Chief Thomas held up his hand. Angrily he said to DeeDee, "Don't go there, DeeDee. Don't even think about it. Francine is here at my request and if anyone -- including you -- has a problem with that see me in my office."

Smiling politely, Francine knew they didn't have a chance in hell of getting her thrown off the Task Force, especially because of her renewed relationship with Mac.

Francine listened as Mac said that she will be the liaison between the Sunset Beach P.D. and the FBI and that her expertise is in profiling. He explained that her experience with the FBI's Academy of Behavior Science Unit in Quantico is invaluable."

DeeDee turned to Chris Burns and whispered, "Profiling is like polygraphs, neither is accepted in a court of law." Chris just smiled.

Chief looked towards the door as Assistant Chief Jimmie Kirk entered saying apologetically, "Sorry, I'm late, but I've been fielding questions from frightened residents. Those pain-in-the-ass press reporters and every politician south of Georgia." The Assistant Chief's field of expertise is just what he has been doing all day. Fielding questions and exuding charm. He has a talent for giving out a great deal of information without actually saying anything. This gift is priceless in dealing with the public.

Looking around the room he asked, "Where's Detective Russo? Did the press scare him off?"

"No, he had to drive back to Lee County earlier today. His son underwent surgery last night. Seems he had a nasty fall and broke his leg," the Chief responded. "Francine, why don't you start the ball rolling?" the Chief suggested.

"Sure. The Bureau has recently developed a new unit at the Academy. It was established when profiling became a necessity rather than a rare occurrence. During the Son of Sam murders and the Ted Bundy reign of terror, it became evident that research on serial killers was a must. Therefore, a division called UNSUB was formed."

Francine stood in front of the conference blackboard and wrote UNSUB in large letters. "This is an acronym for UNidentified SUBject," speaking as she wrote it out. "After intensive research we developed a formula for identifying suspects. Breaking down and categorizing the information it leads to WHY + HOW = WHO. By examining the behavioral evidence at a crime scene, in the statements from witnesses or in the autopsy reports, a definite pattern emerges.

One. Most serial killers come from dysfunctional backgrounds and the majority have suffered from physical and or sexual abuse." Francine was pleased the Task Force members were using the pads in front of them for more than just doodling.

"Two. These killers are from alcoholic and or drug using parents or guardians and have lived in a multitude of homes." Holding up her hand Francine proceeded to three. "Serial killers plan their attacks. Depending on the way the body is found, we can determine the mental state of the killer. For instance, your body is found wrapped in a blanket that suggests, to us, that the killer had some tender feelings toward the victim. He or she might even feel remorse.

Another so-called influencing or mitigating factor that's come to the forefront is the media. Do people really get ideas for crimes from watching TV or imitating something they see in the movies? There's no proof either way. Why can 20 million people watch a TV program and only one of them copy the plot and actually kill someone?"

Francine finished up by extolling the advantages of partnering with the Bureau and then turned it over to the Chief as she returned to her chair.

"Good job, Francine; thanks. Tina, you're next."

Referring to her notes, Tina confirmed, "All forensic evidence points toward a serial killer. The angle of the head, the way the neck was broken, identical in all three homicides. All three victims were covered with a pink blanket. The fibers from the blankets indicate that they are from the same dye-lot. The most convincing piece of evidence is that in all three homicides, the victims wore scarves and their shoes and handbags were taken from the scene."

Sgt. Burns interrupted, "Why don't we each take a specific area of each of these homicides to investigate? This will eliminate the possibilities of more than one detective covering the same ground."

The group nodded their approval and Chief Thomas began handing out assignments according to the expertise of the Task Force member.

"Francine will work on compiling the information needed to feed into the computers and start profiling the suspect. Nick will coordinate the homicides between the Lee County Sheriff's Office and the Sunset Beach Police Department. Chris Burns will be responsible for obtaining all evidence that has to do with fingerprinting, and I want him to be the liaison between the Task Force and road patrol." Turning to the group Chief continued, "If any of you need additional personnel, Chris will be the one who assigns them."

"Let's set weekly meetings for five p.m. until we close this case," suggested Assistant Chief Kirk. "We can always schedule additional meetings as the need arises."

Standing up to leave, Chief repeated, "I don't want anyone, that means anyone, working this case to speak to any member of the media without written consent. That's why we pay a PIO. And if I find out who dropped the dime to the media that started this panic this morning, they will wish they were never born."

Jeannine, the Chief's assistant, buzzed, "Chief, your wife's on the phone."

"Let's take a break," he said as he excused himself to take the call.

Picking up the phone he asked, "Are you all right? The kids OK?" He knew something was up because she never interrupted him when he was in a meeting.

"My brother, Joe, just called. Mom was taken to Orlando General complaining of chest pains. I'm catching the six-ten to Orlando. I'll call you when I know what's happening. Don't worry about the kids. I called your sister, and she's going to take them for a few days. You've got enough on your plate right now and anyway you know how they love being with your sister. They won't miss either one of us," she said with a chuckle.

"Ellen, that's just like you to be worrying about me, but what can I do for you? I always tell my staff that family comes first before the job, and you know I mean that. If you want me to be with you and Mom, call me. Give your Mom a kiss for me."

Re-entering the room the Task Force took their seats. Making sure there were no pressing questions and that everyone has their notes and assignments, Thomas adjourned the meeting. "See you tomorrow at five," he said as he headed for the door.

Chapter Four
Monday, February 4th

Pam, Maxine and Judy arrived at the Clubhouse, headed for the dining room and their usual table and found that Beth was already seated.

After each had ordered her favorite salad along with iced tea, they all started to talk at once about the possibility of a serial killer stalking senior women in Sunset Beach.

"Have the police released anything new?" asked Pam.

Maxine answered with a shake of her head while Judy exclaimed, "Oh my God, that woman lived right down the street from us."

"I'm sure the police have everything under control," Maxine said.

Pam chimed in, "They can't catch this guy fast enough to suit me."

"Enough about this murder. Doesn't anyone want to hear about my big date with Allan last night?" interrupted an annoyed Beth.

"Of course we do," Judy said. "But I'm really scared. That woman was a neighbor, even if I didn't know her personally." Facing Maxine she asked, "Can you call your friend Phyllis at the police department and get the low down on what's really happening?"

Maxine answered, "Sure, I'll try to reach her after lunch."

The ladies then turned their attention to a miffed Beth and Pam said, "Okay my friend, you have my undivided attention, so start at the beginning."

Blushing, Beth said, "When I opened the door Allan handed me the most magnificent bouquet of flowers that I have ever seen. The colors were so unusual, let alone that some were exotic! It was quite expensive, I'm sure. We then went to..." Beth stopped in mid-sentence as Pam motioned to the waitress.

"Can you please turn up the sound on your TV?" Pam inquired. Channel 10's Anchorman Steve Weston could be heard interviewing Daniel Wagner, the Lee County Sheriff.

"Well, Steve, we are in the process of comparing the evidence we have from our two homicides to the evidence that was found here on Sunset Beach. The similarities, like the missing shoes and handbags, far outweigh the differences for it to be just a coincidence, though we are not ready to speculate that these homicides are anything more than random murders."

"Beth, what's the matter? The color just drained from your face! Are you OK?" Judy nervously asked. Maxine and Pam turn from the TV with concern.

"Allan told me he lived on Sanibel Island for six months before moving here. Sanibel's in Lee County, isn't it?" she asked with a tremble. "Oh, God, he also admired the shoes I was wearing and said how well they complimented my handbag.

We have another date for this Sunday. Do you think I should cancel it or am I just being silly? My mind is in overdrive. What do you girls think?"

"Well, I for one think you should cancel your Sunday plans," said Maxine. "At least until I can get the real scoop from Phyllis." Both Pam and Judy nodded vigorously in agreement.

"You're probably right. I should err on the side of caution even if this messes up a date with the first attractive, intelligent man I've met since George died." Giving the girls a wan smile she said, "I feel a headache coming on. I think I'll take lunch home and lie down. I want to be okay for the fundraiser at the Mardi Gras tonight. By the way, whose turn is it to drive?"

"Mine. I'll meet you in the lobby at six-thirty," answered Judy.

As Beth got up to leave she saw Allan Grimm enter the dining room from a side door with a very attractive brunette on his arm. Beth quickly headed for the front entrance hoping her friends didn't notice Allan as he sat down with his back to them.

Chief Thomas returned to his office and while lost in thought, the ringing phone jarred him back to reality.

"I'm Gwen Johnson, Joan Simpson's neighbor. I'm sorry to bother you, but I offered to pick up her sister, Grace Fields, at the Fort Lauderdale/Hollywood Airport's Jet Blue Terminal and my car won't start. I called Triple A, and they told me it could take between forty-five minutes to an hour before they could send out a tow truck. I wonder if you would have a way of contacting Mrs. Fields when she steps off the plane?" she continued without stopping for a breath. "She really doesn't know anyone here and I don't want her to think that we have abandoned her."

"I'm glad you called me, and let me assure you that you are no bother. I'm sure we can help," promised the Chief. "I'll have Officer Angel meet you in the parking lot of your building, and she will drive you to the airport." Trying to lighten up the conversation, Chief said, "Don't worry about your getting there late. Officer Angel is lovingly referred to here at the station as lead foot. She has been know to occasionally drive over the speed limit, but up until today the rumor has been unfounded. Maybe this is the day we can finally uncover the truth about her driving. Are you interested in this assignment, Mrs. Johnson?"

Amused Gwen Johnson replied, "No, thank you; I don't want to be known as The S.B.S.S."

"What in heavens name is that?" Chief asked. "Some detective you are," answered Gwen Johnson. "It stands for Sunset Beach's Senior Snitch." Laughing uncontrollably, Chief choked, "Okay, but feel free to call me if you change your mind." Putting the receiver down, he buzzed DeeDee to tell her to raise Officer Angel and have her 10-19 the department.

When Officer Angel arrived, Chief told her about Gwen Johnson and her dilemma and instructed her to pick her up in the parking lot of her building and head out to the airport ASAP. Diane asked him if, after she picked up the victim's sister, she should she bring her straight to his office and then take the neighbor home, or should she just take the two of them back to the condominium. Hesitating for just a moment, Chief told her to take them back to Joan Simpson's apartment and help get the sister settled.

Finding Gwen Johnson pacing in front of her building, Officer Angel exited the car to open the door for her. As soon as she settled in, Gwen told Officer Angel that the Condo's maintenance man was able to get her car started and was going to take it to her mechanic. Then checking her watch, she asked if they are going to be able to get to the airport on time. Officer Angel smilingly reassured her that with her driving they would probably be early.

Dropping Gwen at baggage pick-up, she then parked her marked unit in the police reserved area. Shortly after getting out of her vehicle to stretch her legs, the two ladies emerged and started walking towards her.

Smiling to herself, Officer Angel couldn't help but notice the way they were dressed. Mrs. Johnson was wearing a red and white blouse, white clam diggers, and sneakers; and Joan Simpson's sister was wearing almost the exact same thing. Officer Angel motioned for them to stay where they were and returned to her car.

After the introductions and while driving back to the Condo, Grace Fields spoke openly about her sister. "Joan was just two years younger than I and we were extremely close. This is so hard to believe. You see, we spoke to each other twice a week." Glancing over at her, Office Angel saw her eyes brimming with tears. Continuing, Grace said, "I don't know how I'm going to get along without her. I will tell you one thing: I have no intention of leaving Florida until the bastard that killed my sister is caught." With a determined look on her face she added, "I hope Florida is still a death penalty state because I want that son of a bitch dead."

Hoping to change the subject, Office Angel suggested, "Why don't we stop for something to eat? I'm sure you could both use some tea or coffee about now."

"Oh, that's not necessary," replied Gwen. "I prepared lunch."

Turning to face Gwen in the back seat, Grace said, "You shouldn't have gone to all that trouble. I know that you all have things to do. I don't want to be a burden on anyone."

Grace said, "Don't be silly. I knew that you would be tired from the long flight." Leaning over the front seat, she asked Officer Angel if she would join them. Before she had a chance to respond, Gwen recited the menu: corned beef, tuna, turkey, and fresh rye bread.

Officer Angel answered, "How can I resist? But, before I accept, the decision maker will be if you have Dr. Pepper's Cream Soda?"

Gwen grinned, "Of course I do. How can you serve deli without it?"

Officer Angel smiling said, "Yes, and as long as you two ladies are on a first name basis and I'm joining you for lunch, please call me Diane."

After lunch Diane started to bring the dishes to the sink when Gwen stopped her. "I'll clean up," she said, "so you two can get on with what you have to do. Let me get you Joan's key. I keep it on a hook in the kitchen closet."

Gwen took Grace's hand and said, "You look really tired. Why don't you both come back here after you handle this dreadful business?"

Grace answered quickly. "Yes, I think I'd really like that."

Diane declined, "I'm afraid I won't be able to join you as I will still be on duty." Both ladies thanked Gwen for the delicious lunch and headed down the hallway to Joan Simpson's apartment.

Entering the apartment Officer Angel could see the tears start to stream down Grace's face.

Diane thought, "God, what a terrible feeling it must be to enter your sister's apartment knowing that she won't be there."

"This is like a bad dream," Grace said. "I keep thinking Joan will shake me awake, and we'll laugh about my nightmare. How am I going to get along without her? She was my baby sister. Let's get this ordeal over with as quickly as possible."

Where do you want to start?" Diane asked. "How about the bedroom?" As they enter the master bedroom, Diane told Grace to check to see if anything was missing.

Confused, Grace said, "What do you mean?"

Diane answered, "We are specifically interested in knowing if you can look in her closet and see if there is a handbag and pair of shoes missing. We know that she had these items with her and we have been unable to locate them."

Going through the closet, Grace turned to Diane and said, "I can't find the handbag I sent Joan last month."

Diane's face lit up as she asked, "Can you describe it?"

"Of course I can. It is multi-colored with the old Miami Beach skyline and a 50's style pink Cadillac with young girl in a poodle skirt and saddle shoes posing on the hood. I bought it for her because Joan had a poodle skirt and saddle shoes when she was a teen-ager. It was so her - whimsical, wonderful, and colorful. She really loved it. In fact, she told me that she found the perfect shoes to wear with it. She described them as multicolored just like the bag."

Her face became animated when she remembered that she bought the bag from a catalog. Sharing the information with Diane, she told her that she had paid for it by check and reached in her handbag to pull out her check book. Going through the stubs, she found the name of the company and asked, "Will this help?"

"Absolutely," Diane replied. "This is the first break we've had in the case. I'm going to call the catalog company and ask them to send us a picture of the bag." Tenderly Diane added, "Grace, you're doing a great job. Your help is invaluable. This clue could be just what we need to nab the scum".

Diane then turned her attention to the photos on Joan's night table. She picked up the four pictures and asked Grace if she was up to continuing. Shaking her head in agreement, she began to study the photos that Diane was holding.

Recognizing two of the photos, Grace said, "This one is Joan and her husband, and this one is Joan and her son. I don't have a clue who the other two are. I do remember Joan telling me that she met a man at a singles' meeting, and they were seeing each other. Sometimes twice a week. His name is Allan, and he was new in town. She also said that she met a young police officer while taking part in a survey on the *Fears of Growing Old.* Something about him reminded her of her son. She mentioned that he confided to her that he was having marital problems. That was Joan. Always trying to mother some one."

Diane realizing how drawn Grace was beginning to look, suggested that they take a break and that she lie down before going back to Gwen's.

"I am tired," she admitted, "but I can't stay here. It has too many memories for me to deal with right now. Is there a place nearby that I can stay?" Diane offered to check on a local hotel called the Beach Inn.

"Thank you," she said. "May I ask you for one more favor?"

"Of course," Diane replied.

Grace with her voice trembling asked, "Where is my sister's body?"

Putting her arms around her Diane answered, "She's at the Medical Examiner's Office."

With tears in her eyes Grace asked, "When will the body be released? I need to contact a synagogue that could help me make the funeral arrangements. Did you know that in the Jewish faith, she should be buried as quickly as possible?"

Diane nodded her head and offered to make few phone calls. She promised that she will ask the department to do what it can to expedite the release of Joan's body so that she can have a proper funeral. She knew, however, that because this was a homicide, the wheels would turn slowly.

Calling the Beach Inn, she arranged for a room and suggested that she tell Gwen of her change of plans. Promising to make sure that everything in the apartment was secured, Diane told her that she would meet her at Gwen's to pick-up her luggage and drive her to the hotel.

Too tired for conversation, Grace tried to smile and gratefully told Diane thank you as she headed to the door.

Taking a last look at the apartment, Diane decided to call the Chief to give him an update. Reaching DeeDee, she was told that Chief was at a meeting and would not be available for at least an hour. She left a message telling the Chief that she was taking Grace Field to the Beach Inn and would be in touch. There was an eerie silence to the apartment as Office Diane Angel closes the door behind her.

Chapter Five

Tuesday, February 5th

Joyce looked at her watch and suddenly realized she had not called home since the day before. Dialing immediately she was surprised that no one answered. She then dialed her parents and her mom, Toby, answered. Joyce said hi and was interrupted by her mother who when recognizing her voice became furious.

"Where the hell are you?" she asked angrily. "Do you know what time it is? You haven't been home all night. You didn't even call the hospital to see how Clyde is. Your dad and I have been worried sick."

Before her mother could ask another question, Joyce, in an irritated voice, interrupted with, "Enough with the third degree. Look I'm fine. Is Bonnie at your house? I tried to call home, but there's no answer. Where's the housekeeper?"

Her mother, trying to calm down, answered, "We have Bonnie with us. I gave the housekeeper some time off. Clyde is doing just fine. You still haven't told me where you are. What's going on? Your dad got a worried call from Nick who told him that when he was getting ready to leave, Bonnie started to cry hysterically and held on to him for dear life. She kept saying, 'Daddy don't go. Don't leave me alone with Mommy. She said that I was a bad girl and doesn't love me anymore. I promise I'll be good. Please take me with you.' Joyce, what's happening? Why is Bonnie so frightened? What have you done?

Nick called again this morning and was livid! He said the hospital has been trying to reach you to sign the papers to have Clyde sent to rehab and when you didn't call back, they called him. We didn't tell him that we haven't heard from you all night. We covered for you by telling him that we would take care of it and that you would call him back. Please tell me where you are. Let your dad and I help you. Joyce, we love you. Just let us know where you are and we'll come and get you."

"I'm okay, Mother, and don't worry about Nick. I'll handle him. Since Bonnie is with you and dad, I'm going to go somewhere quiet and try to think things out. I need some time by myself. I'll call the hospital and take care of whatever it is that they need. I'm also going to call my friend Rita and have her pick up Bonnie and take her to her house for a few days."

"Absolutely not," said Toby. "Your dad and I are perfectly capable of taking care of our granddaughter."

Suddenly starting to scream uncontrollably Joyce said, "Don't you tell me what to do with my daughter. You always wanted to take her away from me. I bet you and dad have spent yesterday and today poisoning her mind against me."

Totally shocked, Toby barely responded, "What is happening to you?" As panic set in, Toby shouted, "Oh, my God, Joyce, come home…please."

"Oh Mom! Forget the whole thing. Everything's going to be all right. Listen, I was saving this news to tell you when I see you, but I'm sure that Nick and I are going to get back together very soon. Trust me. It will be like old times. Tell Bonnie that I love her and will see you all soon."

Toby, hearing a dial tone, realized that her daughter had hung up without even saying good-bye. Turning to her husband Eric, she said. "This outburst is terrifying. She wouldn't even tell me where she is or where she spent the night. Then she told me that she and Nick are getting back together. Oh Eric, she's frightening the hell out of me. Maybe we should call her doctor. It's obvious that her meds aren't working."

He then put his arms around her and trying to comfort her said, "Toby, first we need to call Nick. This time I think she's in serious trouble and we're going to need his help."

Chapter Six
Wednesday, Februay 6th

Chief Thomas heading for his garage paused to pick up the ringing phone. Hearing Phyllis' voice he said, "It's eleven thirty. Didn't you remember that I said I would be coming in late?"

"Yes, Chief, I did, but I just got the strangest phone call from a woman telling me about a white female covered with a pink blanket lying on the beach. Then she said it looked like a signal seven and hung up. I tried our caller ID but it came up "Blocked."

"You're sure her precise words were *signal seven*?"

"Yeah, that's why I called you right away. The location she gave is right near where Joan Simpson's body was found. Oh, and one more thing, her shoes and handbag are missing. Why would she mention that? And how would she know what a signal seven is?"

How would she, is exactly what Chief is wondering. "Phyllis, beep the Task Force and have them 10-18 the station within the hour, preferably within a half hour. Then call

Francine Bolton at the Bureau's North Miami Office, Detective Nick Russo at the Lee County Sheriff's Office and Tina Lange. Their cell numbers are in my rolodex."

"Do you want me to call the City Manager, the Mayor, and the City Commissioners?" Phyllis questioned.

"No. I'll make the other calls including Assistant Chief Kirk. You get started and I'll be in shortly," grumbled the Chief.

Phyllis reached Francine first. "Chief Thomas wants all Task Force members at the station within the hour, sooner if possible."

"I'm on my way," answered Francine.

Reaching Nick, Phyllis told him the same thing.

"I'll be there," he said.

She then called Tina Lange who responded, "I can be there within the hour."

Still at home Mac reached Assistant Chief Kirk and quickly got to the reason for the call. "Jimmie," he said, "the shit's hit the fan. Another body's been found."

Jimmie reassured him that he was on his way and that everything would work out as it always does.

Calling the City Manager, Mac gave him the same information he'd just given the Assistant Chief. Asking him to call the Mayor and the City Commissioners, they agreed to meet at the department in twenty minutes.

Now, for the really tough call he thinks, as he places a call to Ellen's cell. "What's wrong?" she asked immediately upon hearing Mac's voice. "Are you alright?"

Mac started to answer when Ellen said, "I know something's wrong. I can hear it in the tone of your voice."

Smiling, Mac realized just how well Ellen really knew him. "I'm sorry, Hon, I can't make it to Orlando. There's been another homicide. I'm heading for the department right after we hang up."

Ellen said, "Mac, Mom is starting to feel better so I'm coming home. You do what you need to do, and don't worry about me or the kids."

"No, Ellen, you stay with your mom. I'll buzz my sister. I'm sure she's heard what's going on, and I'll ask her if she can keep the kids a few days longer. Don't be concerned about me. I'll probably wind up sleeping at the office, but I'll call your cell and let you know what's happening. I'll call around ten."

Pausing, Mac said, "Ellen, I love you. You know that don't you? Maybe I don't say it often enough but I do. I really miss you."

"I know you do," Ellen responded, "and I miss you, too. Just be careful and we'll talk tonight."

As he hung up, Mac realized he really meant what he said to Ellen. They shared so much over so many years. She never once made him feel guilty for all the long hours and missed parties she endured so he could *climb the corporate ladder*, as they say. She was always there for him and his career. The pressure never seemed to get to her as it did to other wives and she could always bring him back to center.

What the hell is wrong with me, he thought? She didn't deserve this crap. I couldn't let her find out about Francine. I was going to have to end this affair before Ellen and Francine get hurt. Shit, neither one deserved this. When the hell was I going to learn that it's not all about me? God, I'm such a schmuck.

As Mac headed for the station, reality set into place and he started to focus on the homicide.

Pulling into the station the Chief saw the parking lot was jammed with satellite dishes and every major TV station seemed to be accounted for.

He could also see the CM standing in front of a bank of cameras. Any time he is in the limelight, the CM is in his glory.

He heard him read a statement to the press saying that *he will personally be heading up this latest investigation and promising the people of Sunset Beach that he will be making an arrest very soon.* Chief was furious.

Chief was finding it difficult to remember that this egomaniac standing in front of the press was his boss. Trying to keep his temper in check, he moved quickly to his side, tapped him on the shoulder, and whispered in his ear, "Your fifteen minutes of fame is over. You and I are meeting, *NOW!*"

Turning back toward the cameras, the CM announces, "That's all for now; I'll keep you informed," and followed Chief Thomas inside the building.

Walking towards the elevators, Chief couldn't help wondering how the hell the media got the information about this latest homicide. Vowing that if it was the last thing he did, he would find out who the hell was tipping off these vultures. Promising himself that when he did..heads would roll.

Deep in thought, he literally bumped into DeeDee. Apologizing he asked, "Did I hurt you?"

Answering, "No, I'm fine," DeeDee smiled at the Chief and the CM. "I thought I would hold the elevator for both of you."

Chief, coming back to reality, asked her, "What are you doing here? I thought you had the day off and were going to visit your sister." DeeDee replied with a smirk, "I was on my way to her house when Phyllis called me with news. Thinking you probably could use an extra hand, I came here instead.

Chief put his arms around her and said, "That kind of dedication deserves a hug."

Laughing DeeDee said, "I'll remember this moment the next time you threaten to murder me because I'm driving you crazy." The elevator reached the second floor and they headed down the hall to the conference room.

Finding most of the Task Force already assembled, Chief started to call the meeting to order. Before he got the chance, the CM pulled him aside. "Look Mac, I'm sorry about interfering with your investigation this morning, but when I tried to enter the building they just kept asking me questions. I felt that I needed to say something. I realize now that I was wrong. I promise it won't happen again."

Acknowledging his excuse, Mac knew that no matter how sincere his apology sounded, if and when the same situation arose, he would react in the exact same way. Once the CM has a camera turned on him he begins to believe he's Clint Eastwood and protocol goes out the window.

Turning his attention back to the Task Force, he got down to business. Making himself clear that everyone will be on 24/7 until these homicides are solved, he told them that everyone will be hitting the streets to follow up on all leads. Continuing, he said, "You all know the drill. Let's meet back here at five." Turning to DeeDee, he said, "Get me a picture of the victim and make sure every road patrol office gets a copy."

TLTL were seated at their usual table. Checking her watch again, Judy interrupted their conversation. "Beth is twenty minutes late. I'm getting worried. She's always the first to arrive."

Maxine reached for her cell and dialed Beth's number. Receiving no answer, she said, "Now I'm really concerned. I don't like this. Let's go back to the building." Maxine stood and motioned to the maitre d' and requested that if Beth Landers should come in while they were gone, he was to tell her to call them on their cells. Thanking him they all then got into Judy's car and headed back to the parking lot of their building.

Seeing Beth's car still in her space, Pam nervously suggested, "Let's go talk to the doorman." Finding him in the lobby of the building, they asked if he has seen Beth Landers. Answering, he explained that she left with a young woman about eight-thirty.

"Are you sure it was Mrs. Landers?" asked Pam.

Trying not to sound disrespectful and annoyed that they doubted him, he said, "Of course, I am. I even held the door open for them. Perhaps she just forgot that she was having company or maybe the young lady surprised her."

Pam still not convinced that Beth was alright turned to Maxine and questioned, "Why wouldn't Beth call one of us to let us know that she wasn't going to meet us? After all, she has never been irresponsible." Maxine suggested that they check her apartment as long as they were there and they all headed for the elevator.

Arriving at the Penthouse floor they knocked on Beth's door when suddenly the door to apartment PH5 opened. "Is there something wrong?" asked neighbor Chelsea Smith as she stepped into the hall. Pam answered, "We're not really sure. We are a little concerned because Beth didn't keep her lunch date with us today and she is never late for anything."

Chelsea smiling said, "I hope I can set you minds at ease because I saw her enter the elevator this morning with a young woman about eight-thirty. I remember the time because I was just returning from the laundry room."

Judy looked at the other two ladies and said, "Maybe we're just overreacting. Beth probably got involved in something and when she checks her watch she'll panic and call us all apologetically."

Maxine was not buying any of this. She said, "I don't care what you girls say, I know something is seriously wrong. Deciding to return to the Clubhouse, they were troubled when they found that their friend was not there waiting for them.

As they entered the lounge, they heard an incessant beep emanating from the TV. The news flash made their blood run cold. Earlier today the Sunset Beach Police Department discovered another body…that of a white female, approximately seventy years old close to the area that Joan Simpson's body was found less than a week ago. The Channel Eight news crew was on their way to the location of this new homicide in Sunset Beach and would be broadcasting live directly from the crime scene. They asked the audience to please stay tuned to Channel Eight for this fast-breaking story.

Without a word, Judy picked up her cell and dialed 9-1-1 and asked to be connected to the Sunset Beach Police Department.

Hearing his phone ringing as he stepped off the elevator, the Chief yelled, "Somebody get my damn phone!" Double-timing it to his office, he grabbed the phone from the far side of the desk.

"Chief Thomas."

"Oh thank goodness I reached you, Chief. This is Judy Fairchild, a friend of Beth Landers. My friends and I just heard about the latest body found on Sunset Beach, and we're afraid it could be Beth."

"Why would you think that?" asked the Chief.

"Beth didn't keep our standing lunch date. She hasn't gotten in touch with any of us. That's not like her at all," Judy stated emphatically. "Also our doorman and her next door neighbor said that they saw her leave with a young woman, yet her car is still in her spot."

"Well, maybe the young woman is a relative who's visiting and has her own car and they just went shopping. Could that be a possibility?"

"No, I don't think so," she replied sounding alarmed. "She would have mentioned having a visitor and besides Beth likes to do her own driving whenever possible. Remember when we all met you and that other police officer at the Mardi Gras Gaming the other night? Beth was having concerns about the date she was going to have on Sunday. No one's talked with her since then."

Chief Thomas' stomach began to tighten as he recalled their conversation and his telling her not to worry. Hoping that this may be just a coincidence, he tried to remember the name of the new boyfriend. He made a mental note to ask Nick Russo about it.

Aloud he said, "Mrs. Fairchild, can you and your friends meet me here at the station?"

With relief evident in her voice, Judy Fairchild answered, "We'll be there in ten minutes."

When TLTL arrived at the station, they were surrounded by the media. Cameras were rolling, lights blinding and microphones were thrust in their faces as they were asked, "Who are you? Are any of you related to the latest victim? Are you here to identify the body?"

Chief watching the monitor of the parking lot in anticipation of the media circus saw TLTL arrive and motioned to Nick Russo to join him, and they headed to the parking lot.

As Judy started to stutter a response, she felt a strong arm around her shoulders guiding her way into the building. Ignoring the barrage of questions being thrown at them they

A Murder 2 Die 4

headed straight for the elevators. Once the elevator doors closed, TLTL let out a collective sigh of relief.

"Thank you, Chief, for coming to our rescue," said Judy breathlessly. "That was frightening. I can't stop shaking."

Once settled in his office, the Chief cautiously handed Maxine a picture of the recent victim and speaking softly asked, "I need you to take a look at this photo and tell me if this is your friend."

Maxine's face drained of all color and then with a gut wrenching shriek, she cries, "Oh my God, it's Beth. It's Beth." With tears streaming down her face she handed the picture to Judy and then to Pam. Each woman in turn let out a sob of recognition.

The brief moment of silence was then broken by Judy who started to shout uncontrollably, "This is your fault, both you and your Detective. Why didn't you both listen to her that night at Mardi Gras Gaming? She believed you when you said she had nothing to worry about. I'm sure you both dismissed us as four foolish senile women with overactive imaginations." Continuing her rage she said, "If you had paid attention to our suspicions, Beth would be alive today. I hope you both can live with that."

Pam, in a belligerent tone, told him, "When are you going do your job? Why aren't you sending someone to arrest Allan Grimm? Get that maniac off the street before he kills some other unfortunate woman. What is wrong with you people? You're supposed to protect us and yet you let this happen." She began to sob hysterically. "We told you to listen to her. And you told her not to worry."

Reaching for his phone, Chief called Phyllis and told her to get a hold of Officers Baker and Angel and have them report to him ASAP.

"I know this may be difficult to accept," said Chief, "but please let me explain the arrest process so that you will understand why it takes time to arrest somebody, so you don't think that we are dragging our feet."

TLTL wiping their tear stained cheeks they sat back in their chairs and listened as Chief began, "Under Florida Law, once you arrest and charge a person with a crime you must be prepared to bring the case to the State Attorney's Office for filing in twenty-one days or he must release him. On the other hand, if you simply request that they come in to help you answer some questions, you have not formally charged them. Then as long as you let them know that they are free to leave at any time, you can question them without having to read them their Miranda rights. There is an affidavit they can sign waiving their rights and it also states that they can end the interview at any time. It's always better to have all your facts in order before pressing charges."

"I'm trying to understand but he killed my friend. I want him off the streets *now*," Judy said. She was feeling a little dizzy and weak in the knees and asked for a glass of water and some place to lie down. Chief, put his arms around Judy's shoulders and guided her, along with Detective Russo, Pam and Maxine, to the Employee Lounge.

Heading back to his office and out of earshot of the ladies, he turned to Russo and said, "Did I screw up? Should I have taken Mrs. Landers concerns more seriously? I remember that evening at the Casino. Maybe we should have questioned Allan Grimm the next day. Talk about mixed emotions." Before Nick had a chance to respond, Chief's phone rang.

It was DeeDee telling him that Officers Angel and Baker had picked up Allan Grimm and were on their way in. Chief told her to have them bring him in through the sally port and he would meet them in his office.

Chapter Seven

Thursday, February 7th

Chief Thomas, concentrating on the to do list in front of him, glared at the speaker as it started to buzz. "Now what?" he muttered.

DeeDee responded, "Raychel Casper is here to see you."

"Okay, send her in and then please ask the Assistant Chief to join us."

Entering his office, Raychel sat down with her pad and pen ready to be filled in on what the hell was going on. Raychel had been with the department for six years, and remembered that her co-workers teased her when she came on board. They would say sarcastically, "You're just what we need here, a displaced New Yorker with an attitude." To their surprise, she was just what the department needed. With street smarts, and a winning smile, the lady from Long Island found her niche in Sunset Beach.

Hearing a noise at the door, the Assistant Chief burst into the Office while expressing his desire to kill the CM. Raychel could never remember seeing him lose his temper or hear him curse and asked, "What has the Manager done to get you so upset? My God, you're red as a beet."

With sheer frustration in his voice the AC said, "Why can't he just stay out of our fuckin' business?! Did you hear him announce to the media that he personally will be handling all media requests and information? I just heard it on Channel Eight."

Mac, trying to calm Jimmie, told him that he had it out with the CM and made him aware that he was skating on thin ice. "I told him that if he continues to interfere with the investigation, that I would resign and wouldn't go quietly. I can only hope he knows that I'm a man of my word and that I mean business. Let's all get some coffee and schedule a press conference today for four pm."

The news media began to arrive about three-thirty for the announced press conference. They asked Phyllis where they could set up their equipment. Smiling, she called for a Community Service Aide to escort them to the second floor conference room. When the CSA arrived, DeeDee whispered, "Don't let them out of your sight. Stay with them until the conference is over, and under no circumstances allow them to wander around the building. Understood?" The CSA nodded nervously and started to round up the press.

Calling DeeDee, Phyllis said, "Well, the day from hell has begun. Not only do we have every local radio, TV, and print media here, but we have their national counterparts including CNN and cable."

"You'd better call Raychel and let her know they have arrived," DeeDee told Phyllis.

"She is already in the conference room setting up the coffee." Laughing she added, "We figured out that once they drink Rachel's brew you can pretty much guarantee that they won't be coming back. It's our best line of defense and our secret weapon."

Amused Phyllis said, "I have to admit that she does make the world's worst coffee."

At four pm, Chief Thomas, Assistant Chief Kirk, and the City Manager John Ross entered the conference room and took their seats behind the table that had been set up with a bank of microphones.

Raychel began with the introductions and then set the ground rules. "The Chief will read a statement regarding the homicides. He'll take one question from each of the local media. I need not remind you that this is an ongoing investigation and that specific details cannot and will not be released. Now, I'll turn this press conference over to Chief Thomas."

Reading from a prepared statement, Chief Thomas brought the media up-to-date. "First, I'd like to thank the other agencies that are assisting us in these homicide investigations such as Lee County Sheriff's Office and the FBI. They are all part of a Task Force that we have set up specifically for these investigations, and we are all working around the clock to find this killer. The FBI has assigned a forensic expert to help with profiling a suspect. You all have been informed that the latest victim is a sixty-five to seventy-five year old white female that was found in the same vicinity as the first victim, Joan Simpson. Though the position of the body appears to be similar, the ME has not completed all of her tests. As soon as she releases the cause of death, we will get back to you. Now I'll take questions."

"Do you have the identity of this latest victim?"

"We have an initial identity but you know we can't release the name until we've notified the next of kin. You folks in the media could help by letting the public know the number they can call if they have any information regarding these homicides."

"Channel 14. Any information on the blankets?"

Assistant Chief Kirk took the question. "We are in the process of contacting the different manufacturers and their suppliers and hope to get some information very soon."

"CNN, sir. Can you tell us anything about the missing handbags?"

"At this point in the investigation we have not been able to find anyone who can identify the missing articles. We hope that one of the victims' family members might be able to help us," said Chief.

Standing up quickly before another question could be asked, the CM said, "I want to thank everyone for your cooperation in reporting this investigation, and to let you know that the Sunset Beach Police Department will bring this murderer to justice."

As he and the Chiefs start to exit the room, the CM turned back saying, "Feel free to help yourselves to the coffee. Just remember that Raychel made it so...drink at your own risk."

The room broke into laughter. Raychel taking this good natured ribbing in stride, thought to herself, "God, the CM sure knows how to work a room. Why the hell doesn't he do it more often instead of constantly putting his foot in his mouth?"

The Chief returned to his office and picked up his ringing phone.

"Chief Thomas, this is Archie Rapkey, President of Crime Watch. We have called a special board meeting regarding the two recent homicides, and we'd like you to be there to answer some questions."

Thinking to himself, "This is just what I need to finish this day, More aggravation and more questions." Under normal circumstances he usually looked forward to these meetings. It was a chance to sit with the residents, discuss problems in the community and get feedback without it becoming confrontational. In spite of an occasional disagreement on police policy or an individual officer, the members were all pro-police and extremely supportive. Knowing the only item on the agenda would be the status of the homicide investigations, he dreaded the thought of appearing before them knowing that he would be unable to answer their questions. Pausing to think for a moment, a smile spread across his face. What better way to avoid the anger from the board when he wouldn't answer their questions than to have the lead profiler from the FBI address the group?

Reaching Francine, Mac told her about the Crime Watch meeting at seven and asked her if she would speak to the board and joked, "Besides getting me off the hook and actually making me a hero, just think of these residents telling all their friends and family that they've met a real live FBI profiler."

"Oh, how could I possibly resist such a charming invitation?" Francine mocks. "Should I compare other cases to this one, talk in general terms or I could have a Q and A session? Any way you want it done, it's no problem. Trust me when I say they will love it."

Arriving at the department, Francine greeted Phyllis and headed to the Chief's office, knocked on the door and responded to his "come in."

Mac, in deep conversation with the CM, motioned her to take a seat while he finished his phone call.

After agreeing to meet the CM the following morning, Mac hung up. He was about to walk around his desk to greet

Francine when there was a rap on the door. Suddenly the door was flung open and a feisty Crime Watch board member, Lillian Lederberg, marched in.

Not waiting for pleasantries, Lillian began her verbal attack on the Chief. "How could something like this happen? This maniac has to be someone she knew. After all Beth was a crime watch member. She'd never go anywhere with a stranger."

Trying to defuse the situation, Mac turned to Lillian and said, "I would like to introduce you to Francine Bolton, an agent and profiler with the FBI."

At the mention of the FBI, Lillian's personality changed almost instantly. Francine picking up on the attitude adjustment promptly suggested that they start the meeting.

Lillian nodded in agreement, put her arm through Francine's, and walked out of Mac's office as though they were long lost friends. As the Chief, Francine and Lillian headed down the hall towards the conference room the excited voices of the group reaches them.

Entering and saying good evening, Chief wasted no time with small talk. As the group grew silent, he continued, "I know all of you are upset and rightly so. Beth was a colleague and a friend, and if you all will be seated, I can try to bring you up-to-date as to what has taken place.

We all know that Beth was murdered yesterday, sometime between midnight and ten am. Her body was found on the beach approximately 200 feet from where our last victim, Joan Simpson, was discovered. All signs indicate that she died of a broken neck, just like the other victims. Now I would like to introduce FBI agent Francine Bolton. Francine is what is known in today's jargon as a profiler. She is a seasoned veteran in forensic science, and is also an instructor at Quantico where she teaches other agents and agencies on the latest data on how to put a profile together."

As all eyes turned on Francine, and when the polite applause died down, the comments from the men ranged from, "She's too pretty to be a Fed" to "she can arrest me anytime." The women, however, whispered "what kind of a job is that for such a nice looking girl?" to "did you notice she isn't wearing a wedding ring?"

Once the room was quiet, Francine began her presentation on the do's and don'ts of forensic medicine and what behavioral patterns a profiler looks for when evidence is collected. Suddenly she became acutely aware of a woman in the back of the room with tears streaming down her cheeks. Francine asked her name. Maxine introduced herself as a close friend of Beth Landers.

Looking in her eyes, Francine said "I'm so very sorry about your friend. I promise that with help from the communities and intensive police investigation, we will catch this lunatic and put him away where he can never hurt another woman again."

Seeing the strain on the faces of the group, Francine volunteered to come back another day and suggested they call it a night. Each board member thanked her for taking the time to meet with them, and taking her business card, slowly left the conference room to head for their cars.

Chapter Eight

Friday, February 8th

Energized by being involved in a hands-on investigation, Chief realized how much more challenging working with the Task Force was than having to deal with the day to day frustration of administration.

Deciding to relieve some of the tension at the meeting he commented, "Wouldn't it be terrific if we could solve this homicide the way *CSI Miami* does? Isn't it amazing what they can accomplish in an hour, and that's with commercials? Now if we could only get our DNA results back in ten minutes instead of two months, wouldn't that make life easier?"

A chuckle is heard in the room and Chris Burns said "Yeah, right Chief."

Continuing the Chief said, "As for profiling..." he turned to Francine and said with a smile, "I'm sorry, Francine, but it just doesn't seem to be helping. I know it's only a theory and not a scientific fact, or it would be admissible in court. I guess like the polygraph, it isn't foolproof. So let's go back to good old fashioned police leg work. At least we know that that works every time. I've made some notes and want to double check that we've followed proper procedures and we didn't forget anything. Then I'll turn the meeting over to Tina."

Picking up marker he wrote:
1. Uniform Officers: Did they secure the scene according to proper procedures?
2. Did they call EMT?
3. Once the EMT pronounced the victim deceased, did they call the ME's office? Have they determined the cause of death?
4. Who called our CSI unit and which officers documented the scene and took the photo?

Officer Baker spoke up and offered to have all the information in Chief's hands by end of the shift. Thanking Baker, Chief turned the meeting over to Tina as promised.

Tina started off by letting the group know that she had finished her preliminary investigation on Joan Simpson and Beth Landers. The cause of death in both victims is the result of the C-1 and C-2 vertebrae being completely fractured and the dislocation of the odontoid process. Only a direct torquing motion applied to the neck could have broken these vertebra thus eliminating the cause of death to have been due to an accident. The scarf that was found with each of the victims was used in each homicide. The victims died from asphyxiation resulting from strangulation."

She continued the briefing by stating, "If memory serves me correctly the two victims from Lee County died of the same type of trauma as our ladies. God help us, there is no doubt that we are dealing with a serial killer.

Nick, please go back over your notes and see if you can find any similarities in these women's backgrounds. Maybe there's something we're overlooking that can shed some light on what the hell's going on and try to determine what ties these victims together. There has to be a common link. I'm afraid that if we don't find it quickly, there will be a fifth homicide."

Manny, who had been studying one of the files intently suddenly stood up. "Did anyone look at these pictures closely?" All the members of the Task Force turned to the photos in question.

Chris Burns asked Manny, "What are we looking for?"

Giving Chris an exasperating look, he pointed to a spot on the photos, "Aren't those tire tracks leading to the body? I think they look like the same tracks in these other photos." Manny then placed them together on the table in front of him and said, "Looks like somebody tried covering them up but must have been in a hurry because you can still see the outline in this shot. They're wider than a car, more like a van or an SUV."

Turning to face Nick he spat out, "Why didn't anyone spot this before? I can't believe you guys missed this! What the fuck have you been doing? No wonder your cases are still unsolved. What the hell else did you overlook? Christ, you guys have really screwed up."

Nicks' face turned beet red and he kicked back his chair. Letting his Sicilian temper get the best of him he lunged toward Manny.

Chief quickly stood up and stepped between them. Without a word he gave Nick a look that stopped him dead his tracks.

Tina was the first to break the uneasy silence. "Hey," she said, "sometimes evidence is overlooked no matter how careful you are." Glaring at Manny she said, "Haven't you ever looked at something more than once yet never really seen it?"

Manny glaring right back answered, "No."

Chief interrupted, "Enough, let's just get back to work. Manny, you investigate the tracks. Finding a needle in a haystack, or tracks in the sand is your expertise. Let's not lose sight of why we are here. We don't have the time or the luxury of pointing fingers at each other. Let's just catch this bastard and put him away."

Tina turned back to the blackboard and added: "Time of Death"

"Even though we all know that it's impossible to declare the exact time of death, the body temperature and the stage of rigor mortis helps pinpoint the time. It appears that all four victims were murdered sometime between ten p.m. and ten a.m. The stomach contents showed they'd all eaten dinner about seven and even though the pattern of insects that invade the body after death was inconclusive, the rest on the evidence confirms the ten to ten time of death. Last but not least, after examining the body for bruises I was able to confirm that all four victims were grabbed from behind. The trauma to their necks indicates that they all tried to resist and fought back. They were all wearing scarves. Since the crime scene did not reveal any signs of a struggle or sexual assault, we have to assume that the area where they were found was not the area where they were killed."

Tina started to get the feeling that she was losing the crowd and whispered to Chief that there was much too much tension in the room to have a productive meeting. Agreeing with her, he advised the Task Force to review their notes; and that they would all meet on Monday.

As the meeting broke up, Manny and Nick headed for opposite doors without even looking at each other.

Chapter Nine

Sunday, February 10th

Grace, sitting alone in the front row of the funeral home, was both surprised and delighted to see how many friends and neighbors of Joan were entering the chapel. Many took the time to approach her to tell her of their relationship with her sister. Quite a few shared a story about Joan along with their condolences.

Spotting Gwen Johnson, Grace motioned her to sit beside her. "Thank you so much for coming," she said.

"Please," answered Gwen, "Don't thank me. I'm just glad I can be here for you."

As Grace nodded and gave Gwen a smile, there was a rustling in the chapel. Grace turned and saw Chief Thomas and Assistant Chief Kirk entering the chapel. Dressed in full uniform, they looked very official and most definitely handsome. She thought to herself that Joan would have been so pleased with this turnout. Behind the Chief was Officer Angel, who met Gwen's eye with a warm smile and a nod of acknowledgement.

As the Rabbi began his sermon, Grace reminisced about their childhood. Growing up, their young lives were uneventful.

They graduated from Samuel J. Tilden High School with above average grades, married, and settled down to raise families. How could a Jewish girl from Brooklyn wind up as a homicide victim on a beach in South Florida? God, the only beach they ever heard of was in Coney Island.

How could this happen? Why would someone do such a thing?

Listening to the Rabbi refer to Joan as a kind, caring sister, neighbor and friend, she was once again brought back to reality.

Out of the corner of her eye Gwen observed Office Baker arriving with another man and saw them sitting down together. She got an eerie feeling when she recognized the man, but couldn't give the face a name.

Following the services, Grace entered the waiting limo that was provided for her by the funeral home and headed back to The Beach Inn. In the quiet of the back seat, she suddenly remembered where she had seen the face of the man at the services who was sitting with Officer Baker. His photo was on Joan's night table. She started to shiver when she thought he could be the killer.

As soon as the limo came to a stop, she jumped out and ran to her room locking the door behind her. Grabbing the phone she called the Sunset Beach Police Department and reached Phyllis, the dispatcher.

Shouting frantically she said, "I must speak to Officer Angel right now. Please, it's urgent." Phyllis explained that Officer Angel was on the road. Grace exclaimed, "This is an emergency! It has to do with my sister's murder!

My name is Grace Fields and I just saw a man at my sister's funeral that actually could be responsible for her death. He was sitting with Officer Baker and I recognized his face from a picture that my sister has on her night table. Please, you have to reach Officer Angel."

"Alright, Mrs. Field. I'm going to put you on hold while I reach Officer Angel. Please don't hang up. I promise I'll get back to you."

While on hold Grace's mind began to race. What if he's a cop? I've heard how cops stick together and that they will do anything to protect up for each other. Would they cover up a murder? Why did I call the police? Now they know who I am and that I can identify him. They even know where I'm staying. Maybe I'll get killed the same way Joan was killed and blame it on a serial killer who'll never be found. It could be days before my family and friends realize they haven't heard from me and by then they could have disposed of my body. Maybe I should just hang, up call a cab, head for the airport and fly home.

Still envisioning a conspiracy, Grace was speechless when Phyllis returned to the line. "Mrs. Field, are you still there? Are you okay? Please Mrs. Field answer me."

After several silent seconds passed, Grace answered, "I'm here. It's just that I'm so frightened I can hardly speak."

"I understand," replied Phyllis. "I'm going to contact Officers Baker and Angel and have them go directly to your motel."

Panic-stricken Grace started to shout, "Don't send Baker. I don't want Baker. Just send Diane Angel, and hurry."

"Okay, Okay. Please try and calm down. I promise I won't send Officer Baker." Reaching Officer Angel, Phyllis quickly relates her conversation with Grace Field. Officer Angel told Phyllis that she was only two blocks away from the Beach Inn.

Asking her to call Mrs. Field back and to let her know she is on her way, she then suggested that she stay on the phone with her until she arrives.

Phyllis agreed and dialed the motel, " Please connect me to room 110."

Grace grabbed the ringing phone and was relieved to hear Phyllis telling her that Office Angel was on her way and should arrive in about five minutes. Trying to keep her on the line without arousing her suspicions, she engaged her in conversation. Offering her condolences on the death of her sister, Phyllis could hear through the phone a knock at the door. Grace put the receiver on the bed as she answered.

When Officer Angel entered the room, she took the phone from Grace and thanked Phyllis for staying on the line.

Grace, grateful to see Officer Angel, put her arms around her and while shaking uncontrollably began to tell her that the man who accompanied Officer Baker to her sister's funeral was the man in one of the pictures in Joan's bedroom.

"Are you sure?" Diane waited for Grace's reply.

"Of course, I'm sure, Diane. When I first saw him I knew that I recognized his face but I just couldn't place it. Then when I was sitting in the limo, I remembered when I had seen him before. It was in one of the pictures you showed me in Joan's apartment.

"Grace, I'm going to call Chief Thomas so he's aware of what is happening. Then if it's alright with you, I'm going to take you back to your sister's apartment and pick up the photo you're talking about. Let's call the desk for a large pot of coffee while we wait for Chief's phone call. I have a feeling it's going to be a long day."

Chapter Ten

Tuesday, February 12th

Nick was sitting in the Officers' Lounge talking to Sergeant Burns when his cell phone rang. Recognizing the number immediately as his in-laws he excused himself to take the call. The years had taught him that his in-laws never called him with good news, and he didn't want his personal business spread through the department.

Hearing Eric's voice, he instantly asked, "What's wrong?"

"Nick, have you heard from Joyce?"

"No, why?"

"The hospital wants to release Clyde, but they can't reach her. They need either Joyce or you to come in and sign the discharge papers. We offered to pick Clyde up and take him to our house but were told that we are not his legal guardians. Unfortunately, someone told Clyde that he was going home, and he has been dressed and waiting since eight this morning. Could you possibly get a few hours off to drive over to the west coast to and bring Clyde to us? I know you are in the middle of an investigation so we'd be happy to take care of him and

Bonnie. The Nanny can also stay with us until we can figure out what is going on with Joyce. Actually, it will be easier for Clyde to navigate with his crutches at our house since we don't have stairs."

Nick answered, "I'll have to call the Chief for permission since I am temporarily assigned to his department. I just can't take off without his approval. I'll call you as soon as I speak to him. Eric, I've got to tell you, this business with Joyce is getting to be a royal pain in the ass. I can't believe no one knows where she is." With rising anger in his voice Nick continued, "I certainly don't have a clue. You and I will definitely need to sit down and have a long talk about your daughter. Enough is enough. I'm prepared to not only file for a divorce, but to petition the court for full custody of the twins. This time she went too far. I don't think I'll have any trouble convincing a judge that not only has she neglected her children, she has also abandoned them." He ended the conversation by telling his father-in-law that he would call him from the road.

Nick immediately dialed Clyde's orthopedist. As he received an update on his son's condition and confirming that he would be getting his son, he headed to the Chief's office.

DeeDee greeted him, "What can I do for you, Nick? Do you need to see the Chief?"

Shaking his head yes, Nick proceeded to tell her about his problem with Clyde.

DeeDee buzzed the Chief and informed him that Nick was waiting to see him. Chief told her to send him in. As Nick entered his office, Chief asked, "What's up, son?"

After telling him about Clyde's discharge from the hospital, he said, "Joyce isn't strong enough handle Clyde."

He explained that his son has had pins placed in his ankle and is in a non-bearing apparatus with crutches and that he had decided to take up his in-laws' offer of having Clyde stay at their house. Their house is a one-story, unlike his which has the bedrooms upstairs. Since he had to go to physical therapy at least three times a week, for six to eight weeks, and his father-in-law was retired, Clyde would be better off there. It was really going to be tough for Clyde because he was going to need additional surgery to remove the pins.

Chief looked at Nick and said, "I told you when the accident happened that you needed to put your family first. Take whatever time you need. All I ask is that you stay in touch."

"Thanks Chief. While I'm home, I'm going to stop by my office and check on something that has been bothering me. I want to re-read my notes to see if there is anything I might have overlooked."

Smiling Nick said, "I can't believe I'm saying this, but maybe Manny was right. His comments made me stop and think. I have to make sure that we dotted the i's and crossed all the t's.

"Not a bad idea," Chief answered.

"Thanks, again, for being so understanding."

After Nick left, Chief buzzed DeeDee and asked her to contact Manny Lopez and have him 10-19 the department ASAP.

As Nick exited the parking lot he reached for his phone. After dialing Joyce and getting no answer, he called Tina. Getting her answering machine, he told her of the latest development with Clyde and promised to call her that evening.

Finally entering Lee Memorial Hospital, Nick decided to skip the discharge office and head straight to Clyde's room. To his annoyance and frustration, he found Clyde looking very desolate and small in the adult wheelchair and tears started to fill Nick's eyes.

Looking up Clyde saw Nick; his sad little face broke into a huge smile. "Daddy, Daddy, I'm so glad to see you. I thought everyone forgot about me! The nurse said she tried to call Mommy but she didn't answer her phone."

Wrapping his child in his arms, Nick said, "Maybe Mommy shut off her phone because she has one of her bad headaches. You know that any sound really hurts her when she feels sick and she shuts everything off until she feels better. I'm sure she'll feel just awful when she finds out that you've been waiting for her. Sit here and I'll sign your discharge papers and then we'll go to Gram and Poppy's."

As Nick turned to leave, Clyde shouted, "NO! I can't stay at Gram's and Poppy's and leave Bonnie at home alone with Mommy!" Startled by his son's reaction, Nick abruptly turned and saw what he recognized as fear in his son's eyes.

"Hey, take it easy, Clyde. You won't be staying at Gram's alone. Bonnie is already there and can't wait to see you. Even your nanny is there." As he headed to the nurses' station, Nick began to speculate about why Clyde was so upset about Bonnie staying home alone with Joyce.

After signing all the forms and receiving discharge instructions, Nick returned to Clyde's room. Gathering up toys, balloons, schoolbooks and clothing, Nick carried the bags while the volunteer wheeled Clyde to the elevator. They passed several nurses who smiled, waved goodbye, and wished him a speedy recovery.

Once settled in the car, Clyde said, "Daddy, I'm so happy to get out of there, and guess what, I'm starving. I could really go for a pizza. Yep, one with everything on it."

Laughing Nick said, "You must be feeling better. I'll call the Pizza Inn and order it now so it will be ready for pick-up when we get there, and we won't have to wait. How about I order an extra pizza for Bonnie, Grams and Poppy? After all, you and I can finish one off by ourselves. I'll just call them and let them know we're on our way."

Arriving at his in-laws' he saw Bonnie, who had been standing and waiting at the front door since he called. As she ran out to greet them, Clyde teasing his sister asked, "Are you happy to see me or just hungry for pizza?"

With a big grin on her face she said, "I'm hungry for the pizza! She bent over and kissed him on the check. Clyde blushed and made believe he was wiping off her kiss.

The twins began to talk incessantly. The strain was gone from both their faces and for the first time in a long time they looked happy. They also did a pretty good job of polishing off the pizza.

After some video games the twins were ready for bed. Helping Clyde into his pajamas was not an easy task, and Nick suggested that they have Nanny Leslie stay with them until he can make further arrangements.

Not wanting to upset Nick, his in-laws agreed.

Wanting to talk to his in-laws about Joyce, he realized that, like him, they were mentally exhausted from the strain of the day. Neither of them had mentioned Joyce. Nick decided to leave it that way at least for tonight.

"Look folks, I know we need to talk about Joyce. We have to figure out what's been going on, but we're going to need clear heads. Let's talk later. Why don't we have the Nanny stay with the twins tomorrow? How about meeting at my place about two so we can talk freely about what has been happening, without the twins overhearing our conversation? I really appreciate your taking over the responsibility of the twins, but we still don't where Joyce is and even if she's coming back. I need to make arrangements for the care of the twins while I'm away. Even though I know I can always count on you, it isn't fair to leave you with the burden of my children."

Eric and Toby, both subdued by Nicks assertive attitude, just nodded in agreement.

Chapter Eleven

Wednesday, February 13th

Getting up late after falling into an almost drug-like sleep, Nick took a quick shower. The housekeeper was there while he was in Broward County so all that was left for him to do was get a few things to tie him over till the time he would be home.

Before leaving for a trip to the local supermarket Nick, called his in-laws and inquired if they had heard from Joyce. They reluctantly told him no. Realizing that Joyce could easily shut him out if she was having problems he knew that her mom was the one person that always knew what was going on in her life. Their love-hate relationship was one that he never could understand.

Entering the supermarket he hurried down the aisle and picking up the items he needed and headed for the check-out counter. He literally bumped into Lori Hock from the LCSO.

"Hey, how are you doing? What are you up to?" Lori asked.

"Nick smiled and said, "I'm hanging by my thumbs. I've been assigned to a Task Force to investigate two homicides in Broward County. Seems their two cases have the same MO as ours."

Lori then asked, "How's Joyce? Bet the twins keep her pretty busy, especially with you out of town. I guess the idle threat *wait till daddy gets home* doesn't work when you're away. Oh by the way, congratulations. I met Joyce about two days ago and she told me that you guys are back together. We didn't chat very long because she said that she had one of her headaches."

Nick couldn't comment as it was his turn to check out but told Lori that it was good to see her. Coming from a co-worker who is with Internal Affairs, the conversation about Joyce had left him a little unnerved. What is this sudden interest in his personal life? She never even asked about the homicide investigation even though it was blasted on the front page in the local newspapers. Trying to shake off this uneasy feeling, he headed home.

After putting away his groceries Nick tensed up. He was really dreading this meeting with his in-laws because they would have to agree on how to handle Joyce.

Toby and Eric arrived and looked as though neither one of them had any sleep. Seeing of what the stress of Joyce's actions had done to them, he actually began to soften.

Nick showed them into the living room and asked how the twins were doing. Eric told him that Bonnie was busy playing nurse. She ran to get Clyde anything he wanted and he was taking full advantage of it. Clyde was getting around a lot better than they had expected and the Nanny was a Godsend.

Eric then asked if he had heard from Joyce. Nick shook his head no and asked when the last time they heard from her.

Toby told Nick that they spoke to Joyce a few days prior. "She refused to say where she was. When Joyce asked about Bonnie, I told her that I had spoken to you and that you were very concerned about Bonnie. I also mentioned that you seemed to feel that Bonnie was afraid of her." Interrupting in a voice that could frighten the shit out of a person, he said, "What the hell do you mean *seems to*? Bonnie was crying hysterically and her exact words were "Mommy doesn't love me anymore. All she does is scream at me. I don't want to stay with her. Please Daddy take me with you.'"

Toby, in a trembling voice continued, "She changed the subject
and told me that I didn't have to worry about her children anymore. That she was having her friend Sandy pick up the twins and keep them at her house. I guess I lost my temper because I told her that the twins would leave over my dead body, and if she kept this nonsense up, she would live to regret it. She told me I could stop worrying about her and that you both had decided to reconcile and things were going to be the way they use to be and hung up."

Breaking the silence that came over the three of them, Nick said, "Let's get this straight. I have no intention of reconciling with Joyce. In fact I have decided to contact my attorney and file for a divorce. It's one thing to make my life a living hell, but I'll be dammed if I'm going to allow her to do it to the twins. Enough is enough."

Nick then turned to his in-laws and wanting to end this discussion before it turned ugly said, "Look, I have to get back to the department. I have some paperwork that I have to go through. Why don't I stop by the house before I leave so I can see the twins and kiss them good-bye?" Toby and Eric agreed and started to head home. Nick drove to the LCSO.

Sitting at his desk, Nick finally closed the last notebook he had been perusing. He tried to convince himself that the reason he went through these books was that the information in them might just help catch this serial killer; however, he admitted that the real reason he went over them was so he wouldn't be accused of missing another significant clue.

Picking up the phone Nick called his in-laws and told them that he would be there in about twenty minutes. Asking if they needed anything from the store and hearing that they didn't, he shut off the lights in his office and closed the door behind him.

Finding the family in the backyard, and his father-in-law up to his elbows in barbecue sauce, he was greeted by Bonnie jumping in his arms. "Daddy, you're just in time for one of Poppy's special hamburgers!"

Clyde joined in from the chaise lounge, "And his famous hot dogs."

After hugging Clyde he looked over at his mother-in-law Toby and cannot believe how much she aged in just a few days. Making a mental note to go easy on her, he walked over to her and kissed her on her cheek. Her eyes filled with tears as she said, "Thank you for that."

After grabbing a hot dog and a cold drink, he started to get ready to leave. Telling the twins that he had to start back to Sunset Beach, Bonnie started crying, "You can't leave yet; Mommy hasn't called. You have to talk to her and tell her that we are staying with Grams and Poppy."

"Don't you worry, sweetheart, I'll talk to Mommy and tell her that it's okay. Mommy just needs a little rest. So she's taking a tiny vacation. She loves you and will be back in a few days."

Mumbling under her breath Bonnie said, "We're happy here. I hope she never comes back."

Nick turned to Clyde and reminded him that Poppy was going to take him to rehab tomorrow. He promised to call him in the afternoon to see how it went. Clyde trying to sound brave told him that he was going to work really hard to get better soon. Nick hugged him with tears in his eyes and told him how proud he was of him.

Hitting the Broward County line tollbooth, Nick dialed Tina. After three rings Tina's answering machine picked up. Leaving a message that he was about forty-five minutes from his motel and that he would call her later he hung up. Five minutes later Nick's cell phone rang. It was Tina. She told him that she was in the shower when he called and thought that he would be coming back much later in the evening. Nick told her that he chose to leave while the kids were still up so he could say good-bye rather than to leave while they were asleep. They decided to meet for breakfast the next morning at seven am prior to Tina going to the office and Nick heading to the department. Before hanging up Tina told Nick that she had missed him. Forcing himself not to think about Joyce, he realized that he was grinning like a teen-ager.

Chapter Twelve
Thursday, February 14th

Sitting in her kitchen and drinking a cup of tea, Maxine was startled by the ringing of her phone. Picking it up quickly she heard Judy, "Maxine, I'm so sorry to call you this early. I hope I didn't wake you, but I know you're always up by six and I haven't closed by eyes all night. I just can't believe what has happened to Beth. I've cried until I can't cry anymore. Pam called me around midnight to tell me she received a phone call from Beth's niece asking her if she could contact a local funeral director to handle the arrangements to have Beth's body shipped up north. Typically Pam, who can never say no, said *we* would be glad to help. Are you available this morning?"

Halfheartedly Maxine said, "Yes."

Continuing Judy said, "I'll call Pam and the three of us can meet for breakfast. Can you meet in the lobby at seven-thirty?"

Agreeing Maxine said, "See you soon."

Deciding not to have breakfast at the Club, TLTL, arrived at a diner just blocks away from the funeral home.

Entering the restaurant, Pam saw Detective Russo deep in conversation with a very attractive woman.

She turned to the girls and said, "There's one of the detectives on Beth's case. While you get a table I'm going to ask if there's anything new happening."

After apologizing for interrupting their breakfast, she reminded Nick that she was a friend of Beth's and Nick introduced her to Tina.

Questioning if they have any suspects, Nick shook his head no.

Showing her irritation she blurted out, "Instead of sitting here having breakfast you should be out arresting Allan Grimm."

Trying to appease her Nick told Pam, "Every available police officer from road patrol to the Chief is working on this case. It is the Department's top priority."

Realizing that she was not going to get any information from him she abruptly said good-bye and joined Judy and Maxine.

Nick checking his watch looks at Tina and said, "We might as well go to work. I don't think we are going to have any privacy here."

Smiling Tina said, "How about letting me know if you're free for lunch, and if you are, let's try to pick a place where we aren't so recognizable. In other words let's get the hell out of Sunset Beach."

Nick with a smirk on his faces said, "Your place or mine?"

Getting up from the table, Tina playfully hit him on the arm and said, "We'll see."

When he got into his car Nick made a call to Joyce's physiatrist Dr. Howard Grey who told him he has not heard from Joyce. Nick proceeded to fill the doctor in on what had been going on.

After a long moment of silence, Dr. Grey made it clear to Nick that Joyce had instructed him not to talk with anyone about the problems she was having. "She specifically said not you, or her father and especially not her mother."

With the combination of annoyance and frustration, Nick uttered

"What the hell and I supposed to do? Just sit by and watch her self-destruct? I can't allow her to come and go whenever she feels like it not caring that she's destroying the twins with her paranoia. To tell you the truth, Dr. Grey, I have had it. How can I possibly leave Joyce alone with the twins when she finally shows up? I won't endanger my kids, and if I can't get any help from you, the first thing I'm going to do is to call my lawyer to start divorce proceedings and then to the police department for a restraining order."

Dr. Grey apologizing profusely responded, "Nick, I'm really sorry. It isn't that I don't want to be of assistance, I simply can't. Please try to understand that unless Joyce asks for my help there isn't anything I can do. Between the patient/doctor relationship and the HIPPA laws, my hands are tied both legally and professionally."

Thoroughly disgusted, Nick said sarcastically, "Isn't that just terrific. What the hell good are you? Does she have to kill someone before you understand that she's in serious trouble?"

Trying to hold out some hope Dr. Grey said, "Listen, I know how upset you are so I'll try and call her. But we both know that unless Joyce is ready to reach out for help, she won't return my phone call." Without saying another word Nick simply hung up and headed for the department.

Pouring over the updated reports from the Task Force and comparing it to the information he brought from the LCSO, Nick looked at his watch and couldn't believe that it was already eleven o'clock. Remembering that he promised to call Tina, he started to dial the ME's office, but before doing so, dialed the Chief realizing that he should let the Chief know that he would be leaving the building. He hit the Chief's extension and reached DeeDee. She told him that Chief was out of the office and was not expected back until late, if at all, and asked if he needed to speak to him as he'd be calling in sometime this afternoon. Nick quickly responded no and added that he just wanted to let him know that if he needed him for anything, he could be reached on his cell. After thanking DeeDee, Nick hung up and called Tina.

Feeling like a kid who just found out that there is no school, he started to smile. Hearing Tina's voice, he told her of his good fortune about getting the rest of the day off, but Tina quickly bursts his bubble. She explained that she was in the middle of an autopsy, and couldn't get away for at least four more hours. They decided to have Nick pick up some deli and Nick suggested they meet at the Beach Inn at three. Tina told Nick that she had to shower before she leaves the ME's office because she doesn't think that the smell of formaldehyde was an aphrodisiac.

Laughing, Nick said, "Somehow I think you're right. I'll see you at four."

Nick decided to hang out in the department and to let some of the other members of the Task Force know that he was back in town. Choosing to avoid bumping into Manny Lopez, he sought out Detective Arpell. Finding her in the lounge, he told her about his encounter this morning with TLTL, leaving out the part that he was having breakfast with Tina Lange. After chatting for a while, they both headed for their offices.

Attempting to look busy, Nick once again went through the papers he had spread all over his desk. In reality he was counting the hours until he could see Tina again and trying to ignore the little voice in his head warning him about getting involved with her.

Entering the deli, Nick thought that he saw a black van pull into the parking space right behind his car. After placing his order, he nervously walked outside to see if the van was still there.

Finding a dark truck occupying the space he began to talk to himself, "Jeez, I'd better get a grip on myself. I'm beginning to see Joyce behind every wheel of every dark SUV. She is really getting to me." Returning to the deli, he picked up his order and headed to the Beach Inn.

Pulling into the reserved parking space in front of his motel room, Nick saw Tina turning into the driveway, and waited for her to park. Greeting her with a kiss on the cheek and engrossed in conversation, they entered Nick's room. Neither one of them saw the black van that was parked directly opposite his room.

Arriving home at eleven thirty p.m., Allan Grimm saw a note under his door. Knowing that they don't allow solicitors in the building, he hoped that it was an invitation from Beth.

As he started to read the note, a look of concern crossed his face. It was an invitation alright but it wasn't from Beth. It was from the Sunset Beach Police Department requesting him to call either Officer Baker or Officer Angel as soon as he returned home.

Dialing the number left in the note, he reached the dispatcher. Asking to speak to the officers in question he was told that they were both off duty and would return for the seven o'clock line-up. Explaining that he hadn't a clue as to why they wanted to speak to him, he told her that he would be at the station at nine o'clock. Hanging up he felt totally drained and decided to go straight to bed.

After twisting and turning for most of the night, he gave up on sleep. Getting out of bed he headed for the kitchen.

Turning on the five am news, he heard the WSBN's anchorman discussing the recent homicide. Seeing a picture of Beth flash across the screen, Allan suddenly realized why the police want to talk to him. As his hands begin to tremble, he spilled his coffee on the kitchen counter and said, "Who would want to kill Beth?"

Chapter Thirteen

Friday, February 15th

Allan Grimm arriving at police department at nine on the dot was met by Officer Baker who escorted him through a side door and up to the second floor conference room.

Thanking him for coming in, Officer Baker explained that he had been assigned to road patrol and apologized for having to leave and that Officer Angel would be joining him shortly.

Finding himself alone in the room, Allan couldn't sit still. Starting to pace and wondering what was going to happen next he was startled when he heard the door open.

Office Angel entered the room, introduced herself to Allan Grimm and then introduced Detective Linda Arpell.

Taking the lead, Detective Arpell suggested that he might be more comfortable if he were seated and started off by asking him if he knew why he was asked to come into the station today.

Sitting in the chair opposite Officer Angel he answered, "Yes, I've been away for a few days, and as you are aware, I found a note under my door asking me to contact Officer

Angel or Officer Baker. I then called the department, and not being able to reach either officer, I left a message with the dispatcher that I would be at the station at nine this morning. Feeling completely worn out, I went straight to bed. Having a restless night I awoke about five am, went into the kitchen and turned on the TV. Catching the early news I was shocked to hear that my neighbor Beth Landers had been murdered."

Gathering his thoughts, he continued, "I can't imagine what kind of help I could be. I really didn't know her very well. We met the day I moved into the building and then had dinner a few days later. It was a pleasant enough evening, but that was all it was."

Sensing that Allan Grimm was beginning to get agitated, Detective Arpell, in a soft non-threatening voice, reassured him that he wasn't a suspect. Putting on a big smile, she asked if she could call him Allan. He nodded in agreement and she saw the tension start to leave his face.

"Allan," she continued, "you know, of course, that you are free to go at any time. I just have a few more questions and will try to keep them as brief as possible. Is that okay?"

Mumbling Allan said, "Yes."

"Had Beth ever mentioned anyone to you that she wasn't getting along with? Is there anyone she might have suggested that you avoid because they were trouble-makers?" questioned Detective Arpell.

Thinking for a moment Allan answered, "No."

Detective Arpell continued, "Just so I can complete my report, please do not take this next question personally as it is strictly routine. Can you tell me where you were on Monday evening, February 6th from ten pm through Tuesday morning, February 7th until ten am?"

Feeling his blood pressure begin to rise, he put his hand firmly on the table, stood up and said. "That's it. I'm done." As he walked to the door he turned and glared at Detective Arpell and said, "I was in Sanibel visiting my niece and you have my permission to call her to verify it. I'll be more than happy to furnish you with her phone number. Oh, and by the way, since we are now going strictly by the book, you can call me Mr. Grimm."

Before he can leave Detective Arpell began to apologize, "Please forgive me, Mr. Grimm. The last thing I wanted to do was offend you." Giving Officer Angel a look that said feel free to jump in and save my ass, she asked him to reconsider and just spend another ten minutes with them. Before he can answer, Officer Angel, feeling a little smug, asked Allan if she could get him a cold soda or a cup of hot coffee.

Returning to his chair he told Officer Angel that he would have a diet soda and that she had ten more minutes of his time.

Detective Arpell offered to go to the lounge and bring it back and then bolted out of the conference room gladly out of Allan Grimm's sight. She collided with Detective Russo who was on a break from the Task Force meeting.

Looking at her he asked, "What's happened, Linda? You look a little frazzled."

Shaking her head she told him about the screw up in the interview she was conducting with Allan Grimm. "Grimm started out being a person of interest in the Landers case. Notice I say 'started out' because if his niece confirms his whereabouts on the night in question, he'll have an airtight alibi for the time of the Landers homicide. He was in Sanibel."

Nick's interest perked up when he heard Sanibel and suggested, "Since Sanibel is home base, it might be helpful if I sit in on the questioning."

Linda told Nick that Officer Angel was with him now and with a smile on her face gave him her permission and blessing to join them.

Nick entered the room where Allan Grimm and Officer Angel were deep in conversation.

Introducing himself, Nick told Allan Grimm that he was from Sanibel Island and there on loan from the LCSO.

Allan Grimm broke into a grin and told Nick that he also was from Sanibel Island. After a few minutes, they began to chat like two long lost friends.

Keeping the conversation light and away from the Landers homicide, Nick commented on how well-dressed Allan was and asked him how in the world he got his shoes so highly polished. He said, "I bet you were in the military. Can I guess and say the Marines?"

Nodding his head in agreement, Allan asked him how he could tell.

Smiling Nick said, "Well, first of all, I'm a detective. Second, I'm an ex-Marine and haven't seen such spit and polish since I left Camp Le Jeune. I had a drill sergeant that was a stickler for neatness."

Allan replied, "So was mine."

Nick decided to slowly bring Allan back to the reason they were there and said, "I can't believe how much we have in common. I'm beginning to believe that it was fate that brought us both to Sunset Beach."

Agreeing Allan explained that he was asked to come into the Police Department today to help with the Beth Landers murder. Nick looked at him with a smirk and said, "What a coincidence; so was I."

Allan now in good spirits chimed in, "Sure, but you aren't a suspect."

Quickly Nick added, "Mr. Grimm, neither are you."

Allan laughing suggested, "I think at this point you should call me Allan."

"Only if you call me Nick."

Returning with the diet soda, Detective Arpell apologized to Allan Grimm for taking so long. She wanted him to know how sorry she was if she offended him.

Allan extended his hand, "I guess I may have overreacted. I know you were only doing your job."

Thanking him Detective Arpell explained to him, "Sometimes people don't realize how much they've learned about their friends and neighbors through casual conversations. Something that Beth said to you could turn out to be the clue that could help solve her homicide. I certainly never intended to upset you and hope that if you remember anything Beth might have said, you will call me."

He assured Detective Arpell that he would be more than glad to cooperate to bring this killer to justice and then he asked if he was able leave.

"Of course," said Detective Arpell. "Why don't I have Detective Russo escort you out?"

Chapter Fourteen
Monday, February 18th

When the Task Force meeting took a break, Nick headed for the door. Opening it he was shocked to see Joyce standing in the hallway.

Flabbergasted he asked, "What's wrong? Are the twins okay?"

Joyce answered, "Relax; everything and everyone is okay."

Nick not able to downplay his anger said, "Then what the hell are you doing here?"

Joyce responded, "Can't a wife visit her husband if she misses him?"

Taking her by the arm he led her down the corridor to the lounge. Finding a quiet corner he wasted no time in asking her, "What the hell is going on and where the hell have you been?"

Attempting to change the subject Joyce said, "Let's not talk about that now, let's talk about you." Continuing before Nick had a chance to ask any more questions, she asked about the progress of the investigation.

Trying not to provoke Joyce's temper, Nick couldn't resist asking, "Since when have you ever given a damn about my cases?"

Ignoring his sarcasm Joyce responded, "Since it's been all over the TV and on the front page of all the local newspapers." Composing herself, she asked if any of the victims' missing items had been found. Nick totally confused about her concern just shook his head no. Without flinching, Joyce then asked if they found out where the pink blankets were bought. Deep in conversation Nick and Joyce are unaware that Manny Lopez was directly behind them pouring himself a cup of coffee and listening to every word they were saying.

Disturbed by how much information Joyce had on the homicides, Manny quickly sat down next to Tina before Nick realized that he had been eavesdropping. While sharing what he just heard with Tina, Manny told her that Joyce had been asking Nick questions about the missing items and specifically about the pink blankets. He told her that the thing that was really baffling him was that the color of the blankets was never released to the press.

"How in hell does she know they were pink? Is Nick discussing his cases with his wife?"

Tina not wanting Manny to see her concern said, "How would I know?" and took another sip of her coffee.

Shaking his head Manny mutters under his breath, "Something just doesn't feel right."

Not being able to shake the feeling that Joyce knew a little too much about these homicides, Manny decided he should do some investigating on his own. Silently he began to create his own to-do list starting with calling some of his own contacts in Lee County.

Making a conscious decision not to let the Chief know about his suspicions until he had some definite proof, he asked Tina to please keep their conversation private adding that he wanted to protect Nick's reputation and his credibility.

Trying to sound indifferent, Tina said, "Okay."

DeeDee entered the lounge and announced to the group that the Task Force meeting was about to resume.

Telling her that he has to go, Nick escorted Joyce to the elevator and told her to drive carefully and that he would be in touch.

Returning to the meeting and after making no headway, Nick was relieved when the Chief decided to call it a day.

Chapter Fifteen
Tuesday, February 19th

After lunch the members of the Task Force assembled in the conference room and were bantering back and forth when the Chief entered. After telling everyone to settle down, an uneasy silence engulfed the room. Chief started the meeting by looking directly at Francine and said, "With all due respect, Francine, I think it's time we forget about profiling and computer images and get back to good old fashioned police procedure 101."

Picking up a marker he pointed to the white board that had been set up in the front of the room and pointed to the four words written at the top.

<u>FACTS</u>   <u>MEANS</u>   <u>MOTIVE</u>   <u>OPPORTUNITY</u>

"No matter how we go about investigating a crime, it always comes down to these four categories. So let's start with what the victims have in common."

A Murder 2 Die 4

FACTS
1. They are all female.
2. They are all in the same age range.
3. In all the cases, the victim's shoes and handbags weremissing.
4. All four were found on the beach.
5. Tire tracks from an SUV were found at each scene.
6. They all were covered with a pink blanket.

Now let's take each one of these starting with means.

MEANS:
1. The perpetrator has to have a job that allows him the freedom to move around.
2. He could be unemployed.
3. He could be retired with, pardon the expression, time to kill.

MOTIVE:
1. Who knows, maybe the guy hates his mother and is killing anyone who reminds him of her.
2. Maybe he hates scarves.
3. Maybe he likes high heels and handbags.
4. Maybe he's just plain nuts.

"Most serial killers in the United States do not know their victims. These killers are like time bombs waiting to go off. We need to find the answer to the question why? What make the perp choose these particular women? How did he meet them? If we are going to catch this sick bastard we need the *why*. We must find the reason so that when he's caught, we can convince a jury. This brings us to motive."

Having underlined *opportunity* in red the Chief listed and read aloud the following similarities:

OPPORTUNITY:
1. All four victims were widows.
2. All lived alone, making them easy targets for a stranger to approach them.
3. None of the victims were sexually assaulted so we know that these crimes were not sexually motivated.

Turning to the members of the Task Force who were all busy taking notes, Chief asked, "Do any of you have any thoughts? After all you're supposed to be the experts."

"Tina," he asked, "have you gotten in touch with the other medical examiners in the surrounding counties? Have they had any similar homicides?"

Tina informs him that she has spoken to almost every city within a 200 mile radius and other than Lee County no one else has anything even remotely similar.

Facing Manny, Chief asked him if he had anything he would like to share. Manny, hesitating for a moment said, "I have a lead that I'm following but it's so far-fetched that I don't feel comfortable discussing it until I have some definite proof. I think I'll hold it for the next meeting."

Nick spoke up saying, "I guess I'm next. If it's alright with you, Chief, I'd like to go back to Lee County and re-interview some of the witnesses that came forward after our two homicides. While none of these folks actually saw the victims with anyone they could describe, I figure it's still worth another shot. Maybe reading about the Sunset Beach homicides have jogged their memories. Anyway what do we have to lose?"

From the back of the room Chris Burns stood and said, "Right now we don't have any clear fingerprints other than those of the victims. We were unable to get any prints off the scarves, but we're still working on the blankets."

Chief looking tired and frustrated said, "I've got to tell you I'm not happy. At this stage in the investigation we should have something to go on. Just remember that the more time that elapses, the less likely the chances are of us catching this maniac. Does anyone else have anything to add before we leave?"

Francine, who is sitting in the front of the room, stood and trying to redeem herself, asked, "When did we determine that our killer is a male? What if he is a she?" Sarcastically, she said, "Since we're going back to square one, I'm going back to my lab and work up a profile of our killer being a woman."

Taken aback at Francine's idea, Chief responded, "That's a fresh new approach, and I like it. Please keep me posted if you come up with something."

When the meeting adjourns, Chief walked to the door and asked Francine if she could meet him in his office, and turning to the group he announced, "Let's get back to work and solve this fuckin' nightmare!"

Sitting behind his desk, Chief heard a knock on the door and Francine entered. Knowing in his heart that the time had come to end their relationship, he decided to tell Francine of his decision. Realizing that the longer they continued their involvement, the harder it would be when it had to end. Mac told Francine that they had to talk.

Before he could continue, Francine interrupted, and looking Chief straight in the eye, said, "Mac, I have something personal that we have to discuss prior to discussing business."

Chief looked up with surprise on his face and responded, "Okay, what's so important?"

Taking a deep breath Francine told Mac that she had recently been offered a newly created position with the FBI in Quantico. Adding that it's an opportunity of a lifetime, she told him that she had been seriously considering accepting it.

"That sounds wonderful," said the Chief. "I hope they know how lucky they are to have you. When are you supposed to start?"

Not hearing the response that she had hoped for, Francine hesitated and said, "I told them that I had some loose ends to tie up regarding the homicide case that I was assigned to, and that I should be able to clean up my assignment by the end of next week."

The look on their faces said it all. They both knew that their relationship could not go anywhere, and this was the perfect time for it to end. Mac put his arms around her and kissed her on the cheek as they walked to the door in silence.

Chapter Sixteen

Wednesday, February 20th

Nick caught a little quiet time at the Beach Inn before leaving for the station but found himself thinking of Joyce. Before his thoughts could escalate, his cell phone rang.

Surprised to hear Joyce's voice and trying not to overreact he calmly said, "You must be a mind reader. I was just thinking about you."

Joyce sounding apologetic responded, "Nick, I hope I haven't caused you any problems with the Sunset Beach Police Department. I know I shouldn't have gone there without calling you first, but I really needed to see you. I didn't tell you the whole truth about why I was there. I know that everything that has gone wrong in our marriage this past year has been my fault, and I'm so sorry for all the trouble I've caused. I just don't seem to have any self-control. I'm experiencing blackouts and I can't remember large blocks of time. I don't know what's happening to me. Oh, my God, Nick I'm so frightened! Please help me! I'm totally falling apart."

When he asked Joyce if she had called Dr. Grey, Joyce answered, "No, he's been no help."

Nick hearing the anxiety in her voice still tried to keep his composure and asked, "Joyce, where are you?" Not getting an answer he repeated, "Please tell me where you are. I'm really worried about you and so are your folks."

With her voice bordering on hysteria, Joyce said, "If I tell you where I am, you have to promise not to tell anyone... especially my mother. I simply can't deal with her right now."

Trying to appease her, Nick agreed to keep her whereabouts just between the two of them. Joyce told Nick that she was visiting with a girlfriend in Naples, but when he asked who, she avoided the question saying she will be coming home on Friday and to please meet her at their house so they can try to figure out how to get her some help.

Nick told her that he would speak to Chief Thomas and get back to her and to please keep her cell phone on. Giving him the excuse that she had been having problems with her phone, Joyce told Nick that she would contact him. Telling him not to worry, the line went dead.

Not being able to make heads or tails out of their conversation, Nick decided to call Tina. Relieved to find her at home he told Tina about his latest phone call from Joyce and explained that the reason he was calling her to discuss his problems was that she was a good listener and a great friend.

Silent for a few seconds, Tina offered to pick him up at his motel and suggested that they take a walk on the beach. "Maybe, just maybe," she said, "we can find a solution to your problems. See you in about ten minutes."

Jumping at the chance to get out of his motel room and grateful for her idea to head to the beach, he told her that he would meet her in the lobby. As he left his room, Nick saw a black van parked opposite his room. Thinking it's Joyce, his heart skipped a beat. But, after taking a closer look, he realized that the van wasn't Joyce's. Shaking his head he began to think that Joyce is not the only one who should see a shrink for paranoia. Maybe he should make an appointment as well.

Tina entered the Beach Inn parking lot as Nick closed the door to his room. Pulling along side of him, she rolled down her window and said, "Hey, good looking, going my way?"

"You bet!"

"Then get in and we'll find a place to shut out the rest of the world."

Nick trying to lighten the subject said, "Please don't tell me you're going to drive."

Opening the door she said, "Get your ass in here and fasten your seat belt. You're in for a bumpy ride." As Nick fastened his seat belt Tina spitefully gunned the gas pedal throwing Nick back against his seat and started to laugh.

Tina pulled into a municipal parking lot off A1A. They walked towards the beach hand in hand. They found a secluded section of the beach and felt as though they were the last two people left on earth. They removed their shoes and continued to walk on the sand. After a while, Nick turned to Tina and told her that he didn't understand what was happening to Joyce.

Tina decided to break her word to Manny and told him of their conversation and Manny's suspicions regarding Joyce. Nick reeling as though someone has just knock the wind out of him asked Tina to try and remember exactly what Manny said. She said that he had concerns about the questions that Joyce was asking about the missing articles of clothing, but his antenna really went up when she knew that the color of the blankets was pink. Trying not to show how upset he was, Nick asked Tina if she wouldn't mind if they called it a day.

Tina answered, "Yes, I understand." They stopped to put on their shoes and silently walked back to the lot where she had parked the car.

Driving in the now almost awkward silence, they arrived at Nick's motel. Before Tina had a chance to get out of the car, Nick said, "Tina, please forgive me if I don't invite you in. I have so many things I have to sort out. I'm really hoping that you understand why I need to be alone right now. This thing with Joyce has just knocked me for a loop. I need some time to think things through."

Trying to sound supportive, Tina whispered, "Of course." She leaned over, kissed Nick on the cheek, and reminded him that she was only a phone call away. Nick watching her leave from his doorway, thought that he couldn't allow her to get involved in this shit. She's really getting to be someone I want in my life. I'm going to have to cool this for awhile and he closed his door.

Chapter Seventeen

Thursday, February 20th

Crystal Kaye sitting at her desk at the WSBN newsroom pulled up her email to check. Finding a message from the station manager, she saw that he had assigned her to the press conference being held at the Sunset Beach Police Department at four pm that day.

Believing that this could be the perfect time for her to visit her favorite Aunt Maxine, who lived only five minutes away from the Police Department, she dialed her number. Delighted when Maxine picked up the phone, Crystal asked her if she was available that afternoon as she was going to be in her neighborhood and would love to join her for a cup of coffee. Not wasting any time, Maxine told her niece that she was thrilled at the prospect of spending some time with her and told her that she can't wait to bring her up-to-date on the family drama. She then surprised Crystal by promising to fill her in on the gossip at the pool regarding the Beth Landers murder.

Crystal was shocked at the comment and asked, "What do you mean?"

Maxine reminded Crystal that she and her friends Pam and Judy were Beth's closest friends and that all three of them have shared the information with the police.

Crystal, jumping at the chance to get a new perspective on the case, suggested that she invite her friends to join them. Maxine beginning to feel very important agreed. Crystal then offered to bring the dessert for the coffee. Prior to hanging up, Crystal told Maxine that she would see her at two.

Crystal went back over her notes on the recent homicides and totally lost track of time. Hearing the introduction to the twelve o'clock news, she couldn't believe that almost two hours had passed since she spoke to her aunt. Realizing that she had another hour of paper work still waiting for her, she put her reading aside and began to write a list of questions for the press conference.

Starting a second list she titled it "Aunt Maxine" and remembering that her aunt and her friends were referred to as the ladies that lunch, she wrote in bold letters after Aunt Maxine "*TLTL.*"

After ending her conversation with Crystal, Maxine called Judy and was glad to find Pam visiting her in her apartment and said, "This saves me from having to repeat the conversation I just had with my niece twice." Excited to share the discussion she had with her niece, she invited both of them to her place for a two o'clock coffee klatch. Telling the girls that they probably could help with the investigation, Judy suggested they write down what happened on the day Beth was found on the beach and all that they knew about Allan Grimm. They decided that this was a lot more challenging than shopping and settled on meeting at one to prepare for the two o'clock meeting.

Crystal arrived with goodies from the local bakery. Maxine ushered Crystal into her favorite room, the kitchen, and introduced her to Pam and Judy.

TLTL couldn't wait to tell Crystal all they knew about their friend Beth's murder. They started off with Allan Grimm. Pam told Crystal all about Beth's date with Allan Grimm and that she was uneasy about going out with him again. She also told her that Beth met Chief Thomas at Mardi Gras a few days before she died and told him all about Allan Grimm and her suspicions. He brushed her off by telling her that she shouldn't worry and to see him again if she wanted to.

"Why haven't the police haven't arrested him?" Pam began to cry.

Judy put her arm around her and asked Crystal, "Do you think you can find out why he's not in jail? All of our neighbors say they will sleep better once he's off the streets."

Trying not to promise anything she can't deliver Crystal said, "I'll try."

Maxine taking her turn to offer information brought Crystal up-to-date on the mystery visitor that Beth supposedly left with the morning of the murder. Repeating the conversation that she had with the door man that morning when he told her that he was sure the car was a black van.

Looking at Crystal, she asked if she thought that it could be a helpful clue in finding out who killed Beth. Crystal smiled and told the TLTL that she was not really sure, but she would certainly check it out.

One thing Crystal is sure of is that none of this information had been released to the press. She can't believe she has an exclusive. She began to plot her strategy thinking, "Wait till I drop this bombshell at the press conference!"

Maxine interrupted her thoughts by saying, "Listen, honey, you had better get ready to leave. It's almost three-thirty, and you don't want to be late."

As she left Crystal said, "I can't believe how quickly the time has passed. Thank you, TLTL, for your help," Crystal kissed Maxine and promised to stay in touch.

At three-thirty, PIO Raychel Casper, ME Tina Lange, Sgt. Chris Burns, Detectives Manny Lopez, and Nick Russo were all assembled in the Chief's office to discuss the four o'clock press conference.

Raychel started off by asking, "What are we prepared to release to the media at this point in the investigation?"

Manny in his own inevitable way said, "Nothing; screw 'em."

Raychel, fed up with his sarcasm, said, "Thanks a lot, Manny. I can always count on you to give me a hard time. You're such a pain in the ass."

Turning to the rest of the groups she said in a somewhat pleading voice, "We've got to give them something before they blast us all over their stations. I can just hear them reporting that we must have something to hide, because we are refusing to cooperate."

"Well, Raychel, what do you suggest?" asked the Chief. "You're the one that has to deal with them."

"Okay," she said, "how about this scenario? Chief, why don't you start off by reading the statement you wrote and then introduce Tina. She can release the findings from the Medical Examiner's Office and doesn't even have to answer any questions because she is not a cop. She could then turn the press conference back to you. You can ask them to show the phone number of the Department and to tell their viewers to please call if they have any information regarding the Joan

Simpson or Beth Landers homicide. Finally, you can take one or two questions and then I can step in, thank them for coming, and pass out our written press release."

Glancing over at the Chief, Raychel asked, "How does that sound?"

Chief answered, "Sounds good to me." Standing up, and looking at his watch, he motioned to the group and said, "Let's go before the natives get restless."

Entering the room that was set aside for the press, Raychel saw all the TV cameras and microphones hooked up and the anchor people in place. This group looked as though they were out for blood today and that they don't particularly care whose.

After Chief finished his prepared statement, he introduced Tina Lange. Proving to be the seasoned pro that she is, she handled the barrage of questions thrown at her with ease. When one of the local cable stations asked her if the rumor that is circulating stating that all the victims were strangled with a scarf was true, Chief came to her rescue, stating, "As of this morning, those test results still have not come back; we will release the results as soon as they do."

Acknowledging a raised hand in the back of the room, the person introduced herself as Crystal Kaye from WSBN. "Chief, I was recently informed that you interviewed a Mr. Allan Grimm. Is he a person of interest in the Beth Landers killing?"

Feeling his blood pressure beginning to rise, and trying to figure out where she got this information, he answered, "No, Mr. Grimm was a neighbor of the late Beth Landers. We just asked him if he had any information that could help. We couldn't interview him earlier because he was out of Broward County when Mrs. Landers was murdered and he just returned."

As the Chief scanned the room to see if anyone else had a question, Crystal Kaye said, "Excuse me, Chief, but I still have one more question. Can you tell me if you were able to find out who owns the black van that was seen leaving the complex with Beth Landers or information about an unidentified woman driving it the morning of the homicide?"

Chief, not being able to hide his annoyance, stared hard at Crystal and said in a clear clipped voice, "That information was not released because it is part of an on-going investigation and I am not going to comment on it."

Raychel quickly stepped up to the podium and announced that was the end of the press conference thanked everyone for coming.

As the media began to break down their equipment, no one noticed Nick Russo, who had been sitting at the side of the room listening intently, break into a cold sweat. Nick's mind was reeling. With the description of the suspect's vehicle and that a young woman was driving, he began to face the possibility that Manny Lopez maybe on the right track. Even he was beginning to suspect Joyce.

Determined to ask the Chief if he can go home for the weekend, he started to approach him but stopped when he overheard Chief say to Raychel, "Stop Crystal Kaye before she leaves the building and get her into my office NOW."

Raychel found Crystal in the ladies' room, escorted her into the Chief's office and closed the door as she left. Not wasting any time or mincing any words, he asked her, "Where the hell did you get the information on Allan Grimm and the black van?"

Feeling a little self-righteous Crystal started to spout the old "I don't have to reveal my source speech" but before she could say anything else, Chief stood up and said, "Let me teach you the facts of life in Sunset Beach. If you do not tell me who's feeding you this information, you and your station will be the last people to ever get a memo, an e-mail, or press release on any investigation emanating from here."

Getting her back up Crystal asked, "Is that a threat?"

Leering, Chief said, "I don't make threats. I make promises. Think it over Crystal. I will give you one hour to come up with a name or I will have a chat with the owners of your station. I don't think you want to put them in a position to have to choose between you and me. Reporters are a dime a dozen but there is only one Chief of Police in Sunset Beach. One way or another I will find out who your source is. You can do it the easy way or do it the hard way. The choice is yours."

As she was leaving Crystal, stopped just before she reached the door, turned to the Chief and said, "Okay, don't get so bent out of shape. If I give you my source what's in it for me?"

Realizing that he had to be careful about what promised, he told her that all press releases sent out to the media would be sent to her station first. Smiling she said, "Big deal! You got me this time, but I promise you that we will meet again and when we do, I'll personally remind you that paybacks are a bitch."

Sitting down Crystal told Chief about TLTL. Shaking his head Chief said, "That figures. Leave it to those three ladies to get involved, but why did they choose you to confide in?"

Crystal smiled and said, "Because Maxine Greene is my aunt. So be kind. I shouldn't tell you this, but they are really pissed that you blew Beth Landers off when she asked you for advice. They also aren't happy that Allan Grimm is not in custody."

After Crystal left, Chief asked DeeDee to please contact Detective Arpell and have her call him. Within a matter of minutes, Chief's phone rang and Detective Arpell asked him what he needed. Chief repeated his conversation with Crystal Kaye and told Linda to get in touch with the ladies starting with Maxine Greene and to find out what they know. "Buy them lunch if you have to," he told her. "Become their friend if you must. Do whatever it takes but get me the information before they give it to the press. I hate being sandbagged at a press conference."

When Linda answered "gotcha" and hung up, Chief returned to the mountain of paper work that was piled on his desk.

Chapter Eighteen
Friday, February 22nd

Waking up at eight am, Nick reached for his cell phone and called the station. Expecting to hear DeeDee's voice he was surprised when Chief answered. Stammering a bit, he got right to the point. Asking Chief's permission to return to Lee County for the weekend, Chief quickly answered "Sure, go ahead. Just keep in touch."

After saying thank you, Nick got an uncomfortable feeling that the Chief seemed almost relieved to get him out of town. Taking a fast shower, Nick pulled on a pair of jeans and t-shirt and headed for the lobby to grab a cup of coffee for the long trip home. While driving on Alligator Alley, Nick tried to sort out what has happened to his life. He remembered an evening about two years ago when he had been working the Charlie shift. He had gotten home around midnight and found Joyce sitting on the floor of her closet in an almost complete fetal position and rocking back and forth. He remembered that when he asked her what was the matter, it took a few seconds for her to respond. She was totally zoned out.

Finally she answered, "Oh my God, Nick, you scared me. I didn't hear you come in. How long have you been standing here?" Before he could answer she started to shake. Out of control and crying inconsolably, she said, "I don't know what's happening to me." Maybe the skeptical look on my face, he thought, pressured Joyce into saying that she couldn't remember anything that happened that afternoon." She then said, "What if something happened like my being involved in an accident and I've blocked it out?" She looked just like a scared child, and he remembered holding her in his arms as she begged him to help her. He worried that he should have listened or done something.

She then fell asleep for about an hour and when she awoke and Nick asked her how she felt, she looked at him with a blank stare and said she was fine and to just forget whatever she said.

Then he thought, "Why didn't I insist she get help? How could I not see what was happening to her right before my eyes? My God, I never brought up the incident again with her!"

Parking his car in the driveway and not seeing Joyce's Durango he opened the front door. Shouting, "Hey, Joyce, it's me! Where the hell are you?" Walking slowly through the house, his concern began to mount.

Hoping that she hadn't done anything stupid, he called his in-laws hoping that they had heard from her. Not getting an answer, Nick debated if he should call the Sheriff's office but before he had to make a decision, he saw a note taped to the refrigerator door.

Nick, I'm sorry I made you drive all the way home but while waiting for you I realized that I just can't face you. Not now anyway. Don't worry about me. I promise you that I will not hurt the twins or myself. I just need a little more time to straighten things out. I'm going to call Dr. Grey and set up an appointment with him. Please kiss the twins. Tell them that their mother loves them and will see them soon.

One more thing, please try not to leave them with my parents any longer than you have to. Don't let my mother make them crazy as she did me at that age and whether you recognize it or not my dad isn't much help when it comes to bucking her. His motto is peace at any price so he will always give in.

I'm sorry for doing this to you and promise to make it up to you. I'll be in touch soon.

After re-reading the note, Nick reached his father-in-law on his cell and Eric asked, "What's wrong? Has something happened to Joyce?" Before Nick told him that he didn't know where Joyce was, he asked Eric where he was and if the twins were with him. Eric told Nick that he was with Toby, Bonnie and Clyde and that they are on their way home. After asking how the twins were, Nick told Eric not to let the twins know that he was on the phone and proceeded to tell him about the call he received from Joyce begging him to meet her at the house.

"I got here about ten minutes ago but she was gone. She left me a note. Look this can't be discussed over phone. Can you get the Nanny to stay with the twins this afternoon, and you and Toby meet me at my apartment? Eric, she's in deep trouble and I don't know how to help."

"Let me get the twins settled," said Eric. "We'll see you in an hour."

Hanging up, Nick headed for his apartment. When he reached the door, he heard his phone ringing. Fumbling with his keys he missed the call. Hoping it was Joyce, he hit the caller ID and was pissed when the number came up ***BLOCKED***.

Thinking it may have been Chief Thomas, he called the Sunset Beach Police Department and was told that Chief was out of the building. Nick decided that whoever wanted him will just have to call back but he couldn't ignore the uncomfortable feeling he was experiencing.

After making a pot of coffee and pouring himself a cup, the door bell rang. Opening the door for his in-laws, he was taken aback by their appearance. Eric was as pale as a ghost and Toby's swollen eyes looked as though she hadn't slept in weeks. Oh, my God, he thought to himself, look at what Joyce has done to them.

Not wanting them to see how shocked he was at their appearance, Nick simply shook Eric's hand and kissed Toby on the cheek while he escorted them into the living room. Forced to acknowledge the horrendous strain that this has been on them, Nick realized that the time has come for him to make other arrangements for the twins. After offering them coffee or a cold drink, he told them about the last twenty-four hours starting with the phone call. After he handed them the note that Joyce left on the refrigerator door, he regretted the decision almost immediately. Realizing what Joyce had written about her parents, he wished he could take it back.

As Toby read the part in the note regarding herself she no longer was able to maintain her composure and she began to cry. Turning to Eric she asked, "What did I do to make her hate me so? Was I such a terrible mother? Where did I go wrong?" Eric took the note from Toby's hand, read it quickly, put his arms around her and also began to cry.

Even though Nick has had his differences with his in-laws, he couldn't stand to watch the pain that they were now going through. Trying to convince them not to blame themselves, he said, "If there's blame to be spread around you can count me in. Maybe I should have done something sooner, instead of blaming everyone but myself. I should have insisted on her getting help and if I did, maybe it wouldn't have escalated to this. It doesn't matter what, **should have, would have, and could have**, we didn't do. That's all in the past. Let's try and work together and first, find Joyce, and second, get her the help she needs."

Nick told them that he left a message for Dr. Grey telling him what had happened, but, he also added that he didn't expect the doctor to return his call. "Truthfully, I don't know where to turn. I hope one of us hears from her soon, because I really believe she's in serious trouble. If we don't make contact with her by tomorrow, I'm going to have to go to the police for help." Toby interrupted him by begging him not to involve the police, certain she'd call.

Nick nodded his head okay and suggested that they go back home and that he would follow in about twenty minutes. He added, "Perhaps, it would be a good idea to let the twins know that you spoke to me and that I am going to pick them up for the day. This way you can try to get a little rest. If Joyce contacts me, I'll call you and hope that you will do the same if you hear from her. Can you arrange for the Nanny to be available just in case we need her to stay with the twins? In the meantime let's plan on meeting up for dinner."

Still trying to reduce the tension in the room, Nick said "Oh, by the way, dinner is on me. I'll let you pick a real expensive restaurant. Your choices are Burger King, McDonalds or Wendy's. If you want succulent seafood, there's always Long John Silvers."

Laughing for the first time in days, Toby said "Shame on you. We will not eat junk food. The twins need a healthy balanced diet. We will have Chinese and that's that." Smiling they all agreed to meet again at the Chinese Buffet at six.

After picking up the twins, Nick was happy to see that Bonnie was her usual happy animated self, but Clyde was another story. Seeing the sadness in his eyes was more than he could bear; he knew now that he would never forgive Joyce for the pain she caused their family.

Asking the twins if they have a special place they'd like to go, Bonnie said, "Just remember, Daddy, that when you pick a place it has to be one where Clyde doesn't have to walk. Don't forget that he's still in a brace."

Grabbing her into his arms and touched by the fact that she is so concerned about her brother, he hugged her and gave her a big kiss. "Okay, then how about a movie?"

Bonnie turning to Clyde said, "Let's share a big box of popcorn. Then we'll have room for candy and soda." Clyde sitting quietly in his wheelchair seemed completely zoned out.

Wondering what he was thinking, Nick asked, "Are you feeling okay? Is there somewhere else you'd rather go?" Getting an unemotional "whatever" Clyde wheeled himself to the door.

The movies and junk food put Clyde in a better mood. Clyde told Nick that he was hungry and couldn't wait for dinner. Expecting him to ask what time was dinner, Nick was taken aback when, instead, Clyde asked, "What time are you going to leave us to go back to Sunset Beach"

Nick tried not to show his surprise and said, "Hey, are you trying to get rid of me? I told the Chief how much I missed you guys, and he gave me the weekend off. How about that?"

Bonnie, all excited shouted, "Yea!" But turning to face Clyde, he thought that his heart would break when he saw that the expression on his face had not changed.

Dinner, however, turned out great. They met Eric and Toby at the Chinese restaurant and the twins really enjoyed themselves and ate until they couldn't swallow another bite. Thinking the time was right and everyone was relaxed, Nick said, "How would you guys like to sleep at my apartment tonight?"

Bonnie looked at Clyde before she answered and got a sad look on her face when he said, "I don't think so. I think I'd rather stay with Grams and Poppy. All my things are already there."

Bonnie sensitively added, "Maybe next time."

Trying not to show his disappointment, Nick helped Clyde into Eric's van, kissed them goodnight and said, "I'll see you all at breakfast."

Chapter Nineteen

Saturday, February 23rd

Not being able to sleep, Nick went into the kitchen to make a cup of coffee and started to adjust the water for his shower when his cell phone rang. Checking his watch, he saw that it was only six am and quickly answered it. Even though he was relieved to hear Joyce's voice, he couldn't seem to control his rage. In a commanding voice Nick said, "I have just about had it. Where the hell are you?"

Joyce replied, "Don't give me the third degree and watch that tone of voice. I'm not one of your perps. I'll let you know where I am when I'm good and ready. I just called to let you know I'm okay and to ask about the twins."

Nick, thoroughly disgusted, said, "Listen, Joyce, I'm through playing your games. If you think I'm going to jump every time you call or drive for over two hours so you can start your bullshit again, you're sicker than you think. As far as the twins are concerned, what the hell do you care?! You are totally fucking up their lives, and all you care about is yourself. Either tell me where you are and when we're going to meet, or hang up the God damned phone."

Joyce shocked by Nick's reaction lowered her voice and calmly said, "Take it easy, honey. I know you have every reason to be upset, but please hear me out. I know that I'm putting you, the twins, and my family through hell and I'm really so sorry. I'm finally beginning to put some of the pieces of my life back together. Please give me just a little more time. If not for us, then at least for the twins. I don't want to turn out like my mother. I don't want them to grow up hating me. I want to talk to the twins."

Nick told Joyce that he was willing to make a deal. If she told him where she was and when they can meet in person, he would let her talk to the twins. Joyce promised to call him at two to make arrangements for them to meet, but before he can ask any more questions, she immediately hung up.

Without delay Nick called Eric to let him know that he had just spoken to Joyce and told him about their latest conversation. Asking to speak to the kids so that he can make arrangements to take them out to breakfast, Eric told Nick that they are still sleeping and suggested that he come over and that they have breakfast at his house. Nick told Eric that he'd pick up fresh rolls and would be over there at nine.

After the twins awoke, they were excited to see their daddy at the breakfast table. Even Clyde had a smile on his face, and, when Nick suggested that they all get together for dinner, everyone was agreeable. Staying and playing video games with Clyde and having *tea* with Bonnie, Nick heard the grandfather clock in the living room chime noon. Getting anxious about the two o'clock phone call and not wanting to be around the twins if and when Joyce called, Nick decided to tell the twins that he had to go to the department for just a few hours but would be back in plenty of time for dinner. Perfectly happy with the time they have already spent with their dad, the twins kissed him good-bye and returned to their usual Saturday routine with the Nanny.

As Nick started to leave, Toby leaned over and whispered, "Please call us as soon as you hear from Joyce." He promised that he would as he walked to his car.

Instead of going to the department Nick decided to head home. Trying to keep his mind occupied he began to compile a list of the questions he wanted to ask Joyce. After all, she, above all, knew exactly what buttons to push to get him crazy enough to not only lose his train of thought, but also his temper.

Two o'clock came and went with Nick getting angrier and angrier. By three o'clock, Nick called his in-laws and told them that he still hadn't heard from Joyce. Telling Toby that he would see them at five, Toby told him that she was planning on cooking dinner. Before hanging up she said, "I'm so sorry, Nick, but please don't give up on her."

One thing Nick had always said was that his mother-in-law was an excellent cook. The food was great and everyone was enjoying the dinner, when Nick's cell phone went off. Suddenly there was dead silence at the table, and when Nick checked the number he realized it was Joyce. Not wanting to upset the twins by letting them know that the call was from Joyce, he excused himself to answer the call on the front porch.

Before he had a chance to say more than hello, Joyce said, "I'm sorry I couldn't call you at two. Are you able to talk to me or are you busy?"

Past the point of irritation, Nick said, "Yes, I'm busy. I'm busy having dinner with your parents and your children. Funny, the only person missing from this Kodak family moment is you. As far as can I talk? Yes, I can talk to you. I just don't want to. So before you hand me anymore of your crap, I'm going to hang up."

Without even bothering to come up with an excuse for not calling this afternoon Joyce just said, "I'll meet you at home tomorrow morning at ten and I promise to be there." With that she hung up.

Returning to the dinner table, Clyde in a serious voice asked Nick if he had to leave to go to work and grinned when Nick said, "Absolutely not. I told you I'm yours for the weekend, and you both know, I always try to keep my word." Hoping that they don't ask to sleep over at his apartment tonight, he was grateful when Eric reminded them they have church tomorrow morning and winked at Nick as if he could read his mind.

When the twins finished their dessert and headed for the playroom, Nick turns to his in-laws, shook his head and said, "This is the last time I allow her to push my buttons. If she doesn't show up tomorrow, I will start divorce proceedings on Monday."

After reading to the twins from their favorite books, Nick kissed them good night, and emotionally exhausted, headed home.

Chapter Twenty

Sunday, February 24th

Nick pulled into the driveway and noticed Joyce standing in the doorway. Seeing him, Joyce began to walk towards the car. Opening the door, Nick was shocked to see that Joyce was extremely pale and looked as though she has lost a considerable amount of weight. He stepped out of the car just in time to see Joyce's knees begin to buckle. Reaching her just in time he caught her before her head hit the pavement.

Shouting "Joyce, are you all right?" and getting no response, Nick yelled to his neighbor who was mowing his lawn to call 9-1-1. Feeling a faint pulse Nick began to administer CPR and was relieved to hear the sounds of sirens blaring in the distance. The paramedics taking over the CPR from Nick told him that they are going to transport Joyce to Lee County Memorial Hospital as soon as they were able to stabilize her. What seemed to him to be an eternity had actually been only five minutes. As they began to place Joyce in the ambulance, Nick started to climb into the back. One of the paramedics attending to Joyce turned to Nick, and recognizing him, said, "Aren't you Detective Russo?"

Nodding yes, Battalion Chief Aileen Tecklin then introduced herself and promised Nick that they would take very good care of his wife. She suggested that Nick drive to the emergency room instead of riding in the ambulance. Assuring him that Joyce was going to be alright she said, "I'm sure you don't want us to have to worry about you too. Please drive carefully, and we'll see you at the hospital."

As Nick headed for his car he turned back and said, "Take good care of her and thank you."

Arriving right behind the ambulance, Nick followed the stretcher to the examining room. Just as he was about to reach Joyce, a nurse quickly blocked his path and told him that he had to wait outside. She explained that they have to get her vital signs and that the doctor was on his way in to examine her.

Nick trying to flex his muscles flashed his badge. The nurse checked out his badge, turned and in a condescending tone of voice said, "Oh, pardon me, sir, I didn't know that you were a Detective; so, therefore, let me re-word my statement: Detective, you'll still have to wait outside while we who are trained in the medical field attend to your wife. In the meantime, Detective, you can check in with admissions. I'm sure they have paper work for you to fill out."

Realizing that he can't make any headway with this nurse he gave her a dirty look and left the area. Making the decision to call Eric before he got lost in insurance forms, Nick reached for his cell phone.

Eric hearing Nicks voice asked, "How did things go with Joyce? Is she okay?" Nick told him that he was in the Lee Memorial Emergency Room with Joyce and proceeded to give some of the details of what had taken place this morning. After letting him know that the doctor was in with Joyce, he suggested that he and Toby get there as soon as possible.

Eric and Toby arrived by the time Nick was through with admissions.

Shortly after, the doctor who was examining Joyce came out to the waiting room to let Nick know that Joyce was awake and that he could stay with her while they run some blood tests.

As the three of them start to enter the holding area the doctor stopped them saying, "Let me warn you that Mrs. Russo is very agitated, and therefore, we will most likely be admitting her."

Toby, the first one to enter the cubicle was stunned to see Joyce. Seeing her so pale and thin she began to cry. Trying to hold Joyce's hand, she asked, "Look at what you look like! What have you done to yourself?"

Joyce lashing out at Toby said, "Well, I didn't try to kill myself if that's what you mean." Pulling her hand away from Toby's, she continued her tirade. "Who asked you to come here anyway? Don't touch me. Just get out of my room."

Toby, visibly shaken, ran from the bedside and into the emergency room waiting area in tears.

Eric who had been standing quietly in the corner finally lost his temper. Confronting Joyce he said, "Why do you have to be so brutal and nasty to your mother? Why do you want to hurt her?"

Answering in almost a child like voice she said, "Maybe if you were home more when I was growing up you'd know." Shaking his head in despair, Eric followed Toby back to the waiting room leaving Nick to deal with Joyce.

Before Nick had a chance to say a word, Joyce looked at him with daggers in her eyes and said, "Contrary to what everyone wants to believe, I did not try to kill myself. I wouldn't do that to the twins or to myself and I certainly wouldn't give my mother the satisfaction of dying and leaving her with my children."

"For God sake, Joyce, what the hell is going on between you and your mother? Since when do you hate her so? I can remember when you didn't make a decision without calling her first. When did all that change and what do you mean *your* children? I didn't realize you had the Immaculate Conception."

Ignoring his questions and sarcasm Joyce repeated that she didn't try to commit suicide adding that she must have mixed up her medications. Explaining that she was feeling depressed and had been having trouble sleeping, she must have taken her sleeping pills and tranquilizers at the same time. Also adding that she had a glass of wine around ten, she acknowledged that the combination turned out to be a disaster.

Starting to suddenly feel exhausted Joyce asked Nick, "Could you please come back later? I just can't keep my head up." She told him that the emergency room doctor told her that he was going to put in a call to Dr. Grey. Taking his arm Joyce said, "Please, Nick, don't be angry with me. Promise me that you'll come back. I really need to talk to you," and closing her eyes she fell into a deep sleep.

Entering the waiting room, Nick spotted Dr. Grey. Calling out his name, he motioned to him to join him in the family area. He introduced Dr. Grey to Joyce's parents. The doctor told them that he would meet with them as soon as he reviewed Joyce's chart and saw her.

Although Nick was relieved to see the doctor, he couldn't seem to shake the feeling that somehow Joyce planned this whole thing. He wondered if she set up this charade knowing he'd be there in time to save her or if she really intended to commit suicide. He knew he had to get to the bottom of this and quickly. Uneasily, he sat down next to Toby and Eric.

After checking his watch for the tenth time, Nick started to go back in the emergency room area to see how Joyce was doing when he saw Dr. Grey walking towards him. Wasting no time, Nick asked Dr. Grey what was going on. Dr. Grey told him that after reading all the reports and talking with Joyce, he believed that it was an accidental drug overdose. "I am, however," he said, "going to admit her overnight so we can monitor her vital signs since her blood pressure is very elevated. I also want to observe her as I plan to change her medication. Right now, Joyce is in a deep sleep and will probably sleep for a good part of the day. May I suggest that you all go home and get some rest and leave your cell phone numbers at the desk? I understand from the nurses that Joyce was adamant about not seeing you and I just want to remind you that she's in a very fragile state so please try not to agitate her. I know you have every reason to be upset with her, but if you loose your temper, you can push her over the edge. I'm planning on coming back this evening. I will call you after I see Joyce."

Following Dr. Grey's advice, Nick told Eric and Toby that he was going to call the twins to tell them to get ready as he was going to pick them up for lunch.

Bonnie answered the phone. Excited when she heard her father's voice said, "Hi, Daddy; where are you?"

Nick said, "I'm on my way over to Grams and Poppy's to pick up you and your brother so we can go out for lunch. How does that sound?"

Bonnie hesitated for a moment and said, "I'm not sure Clyde and I can go right now. You see, Grams and Poppy aren't home, and we just can't leave without telling them where we are going. You know how they are," she continued. "They're such worry-warts."

Laughing Nick told her, "The worry-warts are coming with us."

Immediately after lunch Nick told his in-laws to go on home and try to rest for awhile while he and the Nanny took the twins back home. He told the twins that they can pick up more clothes and even a few more toys. Nick reassured Toby and said, "It will be good for them to spend some time in their own house even if it's just for a little while." Reluctantly, Toby agreed.

After arriving home and without revealing the reason, Nick told the Nanny that Joyce was in the hospital and asked her not to mention it to the twins. He helped Clyde into the house and carried him up the stairs. Sensing that something is wrong, he asked Clyde, "What's the matter?" Clyde just said that he didn't like to be upstairs by himself because he was afraid of the steps. Thinking it was because he had fallen down them he asked Clyde if he wanted him to carry him back down to the first floor.

He was surprised when Clyde said, "Nah, I'll be okay," and then asked, "Is Mommy coming home?" Nick watched the fear leave Clyde's face when he told his son no. Wondering what all this really was about, he made a mental note to add this to his list to questions for Joyce. He told his children that he would be out for a little while as they settled in. On his way out, though, Nick whispered to Nanny that he was on his way to the hospital and would be in touch.

Arriving at the hospital, Nick was told that Joyce had been moved to a private room. When he reached the floor, the nurse informed him that Mrs. Russo was resting quietly. Entering the room, Nick found it empty and noticed that her lunch tray was untouched and her clothes closet was empty.

Hurrying back to the nurses' station, he approached the nurse that just told him that his wife was resting comfortably and asked, "Where the hell is my wife?"

Annoyed she told him in an icily that she would check the computer to see if Mrs. Russo was scheduled for testing. After finding out that she was not taking any tests, the nurse researched further and discovered that the patient had signed herself out. Given that information Nick lost his temper and shouted, "How in the hell did you let her leave? Don't you morons check a patient's chart? The women tried to kill herself this morning! They admitted her overnight for observation!"

Incensed Nick punched Dr. Grey's number in his cell phone and told him that he had returned to the hospital where Joyce checked herself out several hours before. Dr. Grey told Nick, "Calm down. We'll find her."

Nick answered, "Don't tell me to calm down! And where are you going to find her? I'm a fucking detective and I don't even know where the hell to begin to look. I'm calling the Sheriff's Office -- and you do whatever it is your supposed to do. I certainly hope for all our sakes that she really didn't try to commit suicide this morning."

Understanding Nick's frustration, Dr. Grey asked Nick where the children were. Nick wondered why and asked, "What?"

Dr. Grey repeated, "The children. I think she might try and contact them."

Realizing that they were home with only the Nanny, Nick told Dr. Grey that he was on his way home. Reaching the Nanny, he instructed her that in the event Joyce called and asked to speak to the twins, not to put them on the phone, and, if she came to the house, she was not to let her in.

His next call was to the Sheriff. Telling dispatch who he was and that it was absolutely necessary for him to speak personally to the Sheriff, Dispatch put him through. Nick brought the Sheriff up to date on his situation with Joyce and asked him for his help in locating her explaining that she signed herself out of the hospital. Sheriff Wagner told him that he will issue a BOLO (Be On the Look Out) for Joyce and if they spot her to call the station immediately. Thanking him for his help, Nick hung up.

His last call was to Toby and Eric. When Eric answered his phone, Nick told him what was happening and advised him that if they hear from Joyce, not to let her know where the twins were and to call him immediately. He reluctantly told him that he had called Sheriff Wagner and that he and his deputies would also be looking for her.

Finally leaving the hospital and still on his cell phone, Nick saw a black Durango double parked near the entrance. Finally fed up with this nonsense, he started to run towards where the truck was parked. Just as he got close enough to identify the driver, the truck accelerated and headed right towards him.

"Hey, Mister, watch out! That van is aiming right at you," screamed a bystander. Nick fell and rolled towards the walkway avoiding the truck by inches. The one thing that Nick can clearly remember seeing is a PBA sticker on the license plate. A chill ran through his aching body.

As a small group gathered, Nick was helped up by a young man who said, "That was a close call. Are you alright?" Before Nick could answer the bystander told him, "Listen, I got a few of the license plate numbers. I'm sorry I couldn't get them all. That bitch really hit that gas pedal. You're lucky you're alive. Boy, you must have really pissed her off!"

"Hey, are you sure it was a women driving that van?" asked Nick.

"Of course I am. By the way, my name is Carl Sands. I've written the partial license number JSR on the back of my business card in case you need to contact me." Getting a closer look at Nick, Mr. Sands said, "Say, feller, you look hurt. Let me help you into the hospital so a doctor can check you out."

Thanking him and taking his card, Nick forced a smile and said, "I'm sure I'll be sore in the morning but right now I have to get home to my kids." Once again he thanked Carl Sands and got into his car. Despite the pain that was beginning to pulsate through his body, he was determined not to let the twins know what happened.

When he entered the house, Nanny took one look at him and said, "Oh my God."

He realized that he couldn't hide his condition and when Bonnie started to run into his arms she stopped short and asked, "Daddy, what happened?"

Trying his best not to upset her, Nick told her, "Like Clyde, I fell down the stairs."

Bonnie shouted as she ran towards the kitchen, using her mother's word, "Clyde, Daddy is as big a *klutz* as you!" and started to laugh.

Nick heard Clyde say, "Oh, no. *I'm not a klutz; I didn't fall; I was pushed.*"

Hearing the door bell ring and fearing that it's Joyce, he hurried to the door and without consciously realizing it, he checked to see if his service revolver was in his ankle holster. When he opened, the door he was relieved to see that it was Toby and Eric.

Toby asked, "What in God's name has happened to you? Did Joyce have anything to do with this?"

Nick lowering his voice to a whisper said, "Yes. Your daughter just tried to run me down in front of the hospital."

Eric asked, "Are you sure it was Joyce?" Reaching into his pocket Nick pulled out the business card with the partial license plate number written on the back and showed it to Eric.

"Do you recognize this plate number? Isn't it the one that is registered to the Durango you bought Joyce?"

Turning ashen, Eric said, "What have we done? I can't believe she would deliberately hurt you!"

Nick, seeing the pain across his in-laws faces, said "Look, Joyce is sick. She isn't responsible for what she's doing. Let's not start placing blame on one another. There's enough guilt to go around for each of us. Just come on in, hug the twins and let's try to figure out what to do next."

After seeing the twins, they decided to try for some privacy by going into the den and closing the door. Going over and over the same questions without getting any answers, Nick realized that this was a waste of time and decided that he was going to go out and drive around the area to look for Joyce.

Toby and Eric offered to stay with the twins, at least for a little while. Then they would go on home in case Joyce tried to contact them. After both promised to keep in touch, Nick left.

Nick drove around aimlessly for what felt like hours. Calling the Nanny he was relieved to find out that everything was okay.

The evening passed with no incidents or news from either Joyce or the Sheriffs Office. After the twins went to bed, Nick began to relax. That's when he started to feel the aches and pain go through his body. After taking some extra strength Tylenol and a hot shower, he headed to the bedroom. When he entered the room, he realized that he hadn't slept in this bed in almost a year and decided to sleep on the couch in the den.

Chapter Twenty-One

Wednesday, February 27th

After spending a restless night tossing and turning, Manny dragged himself out of bed and into the shower. About four am, he made the decision to let the Chief know of his suspicions regarding Joyce Russo.

Arriving at the station, Manny went straight to DeeDee and asked her to please let the Chief know that he needed to see him since something had come up on the homicides, and that it was urgent. DeeDee looked at Manny and not used to hearing Manny sounding so concerned, she immediately called into the Chief's office. Explaining that Manny was in her office, she repeated their conversation. She put her hand over the mouthpiece and told him to go right in. Manny gathering up his notes knocked on the Chief's door and walked in.

Without saying a word, Manny put his papers on Chief's conference table. After a moment, he looked at Chief and said, "I don't know where to start. What I'm about to say is so bizarre that I don't even believe it. Please listen to what I have to say before you throw me out." Getting the Chief's full attention, Manny began to pace. He finally blurted out that he thought Nick Russo's wife could be involved in the homicides and sat down to wait for the Chief's reaction.

Literally jumping out of his chair, Chief Thomas turned to Manny and said, "You'd better have some concrete evidence before we taint a fellow police officer." Waiting for an answer, Chief said, "I guess it's my turn to pace."

Manny took a deep breath and said, "Let me start at the beginning. Do you remember when Joyce Russo showed up at the station?" Chief indicated he did. "Well, from the expression on Nick's face he was really surprised to see her. When they were talking in the lounge, I overheard her discussing the homicides. She knew information that was not released to the public. Now, I know what you're thinking. You're thinking that Nick probably discussed the case with her, and in conversation, told her more than he should have. That was also my first reaction until I spoke to Tina. She said that she heard Nick's reputation back home was that he kept his police work and his home life separate. That he never discusses his cases with anyone -- especially with his wife. So I couldn't understand how she knew as much as she knew.

Chief, something is definitely wrong. First of all, if she is as wonderful a wife and mother that she portrays herself to be, how come she left her sick son and drove for over two hours to see a man who's working his butt off unless she doesn't trust him? On top of that, they aren't living together. Tina told me that they have been separated for about a year. Chief, I just can't put my finger on it *yet*. Please give me a chance to check it out. Let me snoop around Lee County. Sometimes an outsider sees things differently." Looking Chief in the eyes, Manny asked, "Do I have your permission?"

After hesitating for just a second, Chief said, "Yes but be careful. Remember he's a cop and you're on his turf. Don't make unnecessary waves. The fewer people that know about this theory of yours, the better it will be. He's got enough on his plate. I'm going to pave your way by letting the Sheriff know that you're coming and why. Take an unmarked unit and keep in touch. When do you want to leave?"

Manny answered that he would leave after the Task Force meeting that afternoon. Before leaving, he thanked Chief for letting him run with this even though he only has his gut reaction to go on. As Manny picked up his notes and left the office, Chief remembered that through the years, he has learned to respect Manny's instincts but secretly he hoped that this time Manny was wrong.

Manny entered the second floor conference room and found Detective Arpell hunched over a stack of papers. Giving him a smile she said, "Well, I have good news for you and bad news. Which do want first?"

Returning her smile Manny said, "Let's start with the good news."

"Okay, the good news is that the blanket we found has a label that identified it as one manufactured by Home Necessity. All the blankets were queen size and made of soft thermal diamond weave. The color was listed as dusty pink and the majority of them were sold on the west coast of Florida. Seeing Nick about to ask a question and anticipating it, she answered, "Yes, it was sold in Lee County."

Grinning, Nick said, "Okay, what's the bad news?"

Linda answered, "Hundreds and hundreds of these blankets were also sold before the company went out of business. Before closing their doors, they sold these blankets to jobbers who sold them to every K-Mart and Wal-Mart from

Key West to Washington. Tracing where these particular blankets were sold will be impossible. Now don't start getting depressed. I saved the best for last." said Linda. "We sent the plaster casts of the tire tracks found on the beach and the lab told us that they match the tires on the SUV's. This one came from a Durango. We also came up with a shoe print. Since all the victims' shoes were missing, we hope this print will be the perp's. We determined that the shoe size is a women's eight. So as in the fairy tale, find me Cinderella and we'll match the shoes."

Thanking Linda profusely he told her that he would see her at the Task Force meeting and went to the motor pool to check out a car.

Sitting back down at his desk, Chief got a call from the CM's secretary who informed him that there was going to be a special meeting at two pm regarding funding for the Department's special projects, and he needed to attend. Asking her if she knew approximately how long it will last, he was aggravated when she told him that she really didn't know but suggested he cancel all meetings for the day. Agreeing, he hung up and buzzed DeeDee.

Telling her to cancel the Task Force meeting for this afternoon, he asked her to call the members and ask if they had anything new to report. If they said that they did, he instructed her to tell them that he should be back in his office by five and to come by then.

DeeDee reaching everyone and learning that no one had anything fresh to report, started to call back the Chief. Seeing that his extension line was lit, she decided to wait until he was free before taking her break.

Calling Sheriff Wagner, Chief brought him up to date on the latest wrinkle in the case. Reluctantly he told him about the dilemma regarding Joyce Russo, and asked him if he could meet with Manny Lopez sometime that afternoon. Chief was a little surprised that the Sheriff had not responded the way he thought he would. Thinking if it were me, I'd be pissed to the ears if another department wanted to investigate one of my detective's families without foolproof evidence.

The Sheriff, picking up on Chief's reaction, told him, "Manny may be on to something." Continuing he said, "Mac, last night Nick Russo reported his wife missing. We circulated an unofficial BOLO because we don't want the press to get wind of it. Tell Manny to come straight to the Department and I'll see him immediately." Closing with a promise to talk to each other soon, Sheriff Wagner hung up.

Mac immediately called Manny. Relating his conversation with the Sheriff, Manny answered, "Chief, this is going to get ugly." Agreeing, Mac said, "Be careful and call me right after you meet with Sheriff Wagner."

Chapter Twenty Two
Thursday, February 28th

After picking up Beth's mail, TLTL entered her apartment to check on the air conditioning and to clean out the refrigerator. Since this was the first time they were here since the day of her murder, their sadness was evident. Visibly shaken they headed right to the kitchen. As they began to empty the refrigerator, Judy dropped a package of cheese. As she bent down to pick it up, she saw a piece of paper stuck under the door.

Pulling it out she handed it to Maxine saying, "Can you please read this? I don't have my glasses on."

Maxine unfolded the note and read aloud, "Hey girls, don't worry if I'm a little late for lunch. I received a call from someone who wants to rent Barbara Ann's condo. I'm going to meet her between eight and eight-thirty and should be through with her no later than eleven. Her name is Joyce something or other and the apartment is for her mother. So……Don't start without me. Love ya, Beth."

Pam was the first one to speak, "What's this all about?"

Judy answered, "I have no idea. Maybe we should call Barbara Ann. I bet she can shed some light on what's going on. After all she was probably the last person Beth spoke to."

Reaching her in her New York apartment and relating her last conversation with Beth, Barbara Ann told Judy that Beth called her the morning she died. She said that she received a call from a woman who had seen the rental ad in the *Sunset Tribune,* and who was very interested in the apartment. Beth said that the woman was familiar with the apartments in the building and just knew it would be perfect for her mother."

Barbara Ann also remembered that Beth was so excited to finally help her rent the apartment. That this Joyce person wanted to sign the lease that very morning so she could help her mom move in over the weekend. Beth then told her that she was going to go with the woman to the bank to get a cashier's check for the first month, last month and security deposit. She had explained that because she left her check book at home when she changed handbags, she needed the cashier's check, and she wanted to close to make sure that no one else rented the apartment.

Judy in an inquisitive voice said, "Didn't you find it strange that this person would rent an apartment without even seeing it."

Barbara Ann answered, "Yes, but I didn't want to look a gift horse in the mouth. Oh my God, I'll never forgive myself if Beth's death my fault!"

"Stop being ridiculous," said Judy. "You had nothing to do with Beth's murder. It's probably all a coincidence. Can you remember anything else?"

Thinking for a while, Barbara Ann said, "No." Judy told her that they would call her if anything new developed.

Maxine shaking her head said, "We've got to let someone know about this note and our discussion with Barbara Ann. Should we call my niece Crystal or Chief Thomas?

In unison Pam and Judy said, "Let's call the Chief."

Reaching DeeDee, Judy told her about the note and her phone conversation with their friend Barbara Ann. DeeDee immediately transferred the call to Chief and gave him the *Reader's Digest* version of what had taken place that morning. Chief asked Judy if she and the other two ladies could come right over to the station. Chief told her that he would be waiting for them in his office.

Turning to Maxine and Pam, Judy said, "Let's go. He's going to see us as soon as we get there." Locking Beth's door, they headed for the parking lot.

When TLTL arrived at the station, DeeDee ushered them into the Chief's office. Getting up from behind his desk, Chief welcomed them by saying, "How are the Sunset Beach Police Department's favorite Crime Watchers this morning?"

Smiling but not wanting to waste time chit-chatting, Judy pulled the note out of her purse and handed it to the Chief. Not expecting to read anything earth shattering, Chief glanced at the note until the name 'Joyce' caught his eye. Suddenly he felt the hairs on the back of his neck begin to stand up and a tightening sensation hit him in the pit of his stomach. Trying not to let TLTL see that there may be valuable information in the note, he tried to concentrate on their conversation. Not really following their banter, he asked, "Who again is Barbara Ann?"

Maxine, annoyed that he wasn't paying attention, told him that she was the neighbor whose apartment that the lady Joyce wanted to rent. Hearing Joyce's name again, Chief almost jumped out of his seat. Thinking to himself that this was the second time the name Joyce had come up in this homicide investigation, he had to admit that this couldn't be a coincidence.

Chief remembering that Maxine Greene is the aunt of Crystal Kaye, the anchor at WSBN, decided to enlist the aid of TLTL, therefore, insuring their loyalty to the department and not the media. Choosing his words carefully, he asked the ladies if they would help with the investigation.

Pam promptly asked, "How can we help?" The three were thrilled when Chief told them that he was going to assign a police officer to canvass their building.

"I am sure that among the three of you, you probably know everyone in the building. I cannot stress how helpful you could be if you can accompany the police officer as she knocks on doors," the Chief explained. With a sheepish grin on his face and shaking his head he said, "You know how hesitant people are these days about opening their door to a stranger, even one in uniform, but if you ladies were to go along with the officer, the residents would feel more at ease and would be more apt to cooperate."

As he finished his sentence, TLTL all agreed to get involved.

"Just one more thing before we can get you started." said Chief. "Let me make it clear that if any information you obtain leaks out to anyone, it could jeopardize the entire investigation. Remember, this is a homicide case. I'm trusting you not to divulge any information that you either see or hear to anyone, and that includes family members and friends, without the approval of my office. If you can promise me that you will abide by the Department's rules and regulations, I will be able to get your identification cards ready for you by this afternoon."

TLTL can no longer contain their excitement and gave Chief their word that he could count on them. Feeling smug and thinking *gotcha Crystal*, he asked DeeDee to please come into his office. When she arrived, he asked her if she would please accompany the ladies to the front desk and have a supervisor meet them there. Advising her since the ladies will be working closely with the department on the Landers case he would need them to be fingerprinted. Asking if she would mind personally laminating their ID cards, DeeDee, knowing exactly what he was up to, said, "My pleasure. I'll take care of it all."

Then suddenly out of the blue Judy said, "Maxine, why don't you tell Chief what the doorman told us this morning."

Pausing for a moment, Maxine said, "Oh right, sure. As we were leaving our building and on our way over here, our doorman told us that he remembered three letters on SUV's license plate. It was JSR and that there was also a PBA sticker screwed into its middle. Is that important? Can that help?"

Chief felt unable to believe that, in less than an hour, he received more solid information on the homicides from these three older ladies than he had from his entire detective squad in almost a month. Trying to make light of it he smirked and said, "Well, it certainly can't hurt."

As everyone began to leave the Chief's office, Detective Arpell entered. Introducing her to TLTL and exchanging pleasantries, Detective Arpell asked if she could have a few minutes of his time.

Answering in a tone of voice she can't quite understand, he said, "Funny you should say that; I was about to ask you the same thing."

Closing the door and without wasting any time, Chief handed Detective Arpell the note TLTL brought him. After reading it, she saw Chief's face turning a bright red and braced for the tirade which was about to be unleashed.

After a short wait, Chief, trying to hold back his escalating temper, shouted, "You checked Beth Lander's apartment. How the hell could you miss this evidence? I should only hire senior citizens! I just got more information from them than from my trained detectives! They even made contact with a neighbor in New York with information on this case. It's bad enough that we didn't even know the women existed, but she may have provided the information that can break this case wide open. I'm calling a Task Force meeting for tomorrow at nine. You had better get your act together by then and get me some answers."

As Detective Arpell started to squirm in her chair, she decided to keep her mouth shut and simply answered, "Yes, sir."

As she stood to leave, she was confused when Chief said, "And DON'T CALL RUSSO!"

Arriving on Florida's West Coast at about eleven am, Manny crossed over the bridge that connects Fort Myers to Sanibel Island. Seeing a sign that said "Welcome to Richmond" and realizing that he left his map on his desk, he decided to stop at the Richmond Police Department for directions to the Sheriff's Office.

Pulling into a parking lot, he was surprised to see a small one-story building that looked as though it was converted from a souvenir shop. Not only was he surprised at the lack of security around the parking lot, but he was even more surprised when he realized that they had absolutely no security.

Shaking his head, he thought, "Hasn't anyone ever told these people that there are nuts out there that hate cops?

Being laid back in a small community is one thing, but this is ridiculous."

Approaching the receptionist, Manny introduced himself and asked if he could get directions to the Lee County Sheriff's Office. Laughing, the receptionist turned to her co-workers and said, "Hey, Gigi, write today's date down. Would you believe I finally met a man who is asking for directions? And guess what? He's a cop!"

Turning back to Manny, she said with a grin, "My name is Gladys. Forgive me for teasing you but you have to agree that you guys never admit that you're lost."

Manny, smiling, said, "I'm not just one of those guys. If you got to know me, you'd know I'm special."

Blushing, Gladys answered, "Well if you're planning on spending some time in our fair city, maybe I will find out just how special you really are."

Picking up a marker, Gladys traced the most direct route on a flyer and handed it to Manny. Seeing a number written on the bottom of the directions, Manny smiled when he realized that it was a phone number and that it belonged to Gladys. Thinking to himself that she was kind of cute, and knowing that he has a weak spot for smart-asses, he decided he'd better get the hell out of there before he said something he'd regret.

Gladys, in a pleasing voice, said, "Good-bye," and then spoiled it by uttering the four words that drive Manny crazy. She said, *"Have a nice day."*

Following Gladys' perfect directions, he arrived at the LCSO. As he entered the new facility, an alarm sounded throughout the building. He found himself surrounded by uniformed officers with their guns drawn. He stopped dead in his tracks.

A deputy shouted, "Place your hands on the counter and don't move!"

Manny said, "Easy, guys, I'm on the job. Let me show you my ID."

The Deputy told him to open his jacket slowly and seeing his badge and gun said, "Okay, you can relax now. He's a cop."

Manny, hot under the collar, said, "What's wrong with you? Are you guys nuts?!"

Deputy Sultan replied, "What's wrong with us? Didn't you see the sign?"

"What sign?" asked Manny.

"The one that said "NO WEAPONS BEYOND THIS POINT! What are you blind, or just plain stupid?"

Manny, thoroughly pissed, said, "Then how the hell am I supposed to get into the God damned building if I don't use the front door?"

"Didn't you ever hear of calling ahead and letting us know that you're coming? Ever since 9/11, no one, and we mean no one, enters this building with an undeclared weapon. We have the most sophisticated system in the state of Florida."

Manny thought, "so much for the lack of security in this county." Then he replied aloud, "My Chief set up a meeting for this morning between me and your Sheriff. He never mentioned calling ahead. I'm really sorry for losing my cool, but you guys scared the shit out of me."

Laughing, Deputy Sultan said, "Forget it. This is what happens when the brass gets involved. Don't sweat it, we needed the drill."

Showing Manny into Sheriff Wagner's office, Sultan told him to stop by his desk before he left. Jokingly, he said, "I guess we at least owe you a cup of coffee and a doughnut for what we put you through."

Manny extending his hands said, "You've got it."

Sheriff Wagner, apologizing for the mix-up, pointed to a chair opposite him for Manny to sit down. Not wanting to waste the Sheriff's time, Manny began to tell him of his suspicions regarding Joyce Russo.

Emphasizing that he had no concrete evidence, told him that he was sure that Joyce was either responsible or involved in all four homicides.

Sheriff Wagner, not disagreeing, told Manny that Joyce was still missing. The Department has been put on an alert and was out looking for her. Confiding in him the Sheriff said that they had been investigating Joyce for quite a while. He disclosed information about a complaint that had been lodged against her. He then suggested that Manny work with Deputy Sultan, and that he would give him a picture of Joyce that he can show around the City of Sunset Beach.

Just then Manny's cell phone rang. Checking his caller ID, Manny immediately recognized Chief Thomas' number and excused himself to answer the call.

Chief Thomas sounded extremely agitated. He told Manny to finish up what he was doing in Lee County and to head straight home. He advised him of the nine o'clock Task Force meeting for the following morning. Chief then asked to speak to Sheriff Wagner. Wondering what the hell he did to piss off the Chief, he handed his phone to the Sheriff. Not being able to hear the conversation, Manny could only wonder what was going on, thinking that it couldn't be good. The Sheriff finished his conversation and handed Manny back his phone. Getting up quickly, he thanked the Sheriff for his time and told him that he was going to stop to see Deputy Sultan before leaving for Sunset Beach.

Sheriff shook Manny's hand saying, "I'll see you in few days."

Seeing Deputy Sultan at his desk, Manny walked toward him saying, "I'll have to take a rain check on the coffee and donuts unless you have them to go. My Chief just ordered my ass back to Sunset Beach and I'm leaving right now. Sheriff Wagner suggested I get a copy of Joyce Russo's picture from you so I can take it back with me to Sunset Beach."

As he left Sultan told him that they were also having a problem with Joyce, but, because of their loyalty to Nick, they were moving *very carefully* on the investigation. Sarcastically, Sultan said, "Notice I said *very carefully*."

Getting up and going to his filing cabinet he pulled out a picture of Nick and Joyce at a PBA function and handed it to Manny. Manny told him that the Sheriff suggested that they work this case together and told him that he'd be back in a few days.

Chapter Twenty-Three

Friday, March 1st,

After kissing the twins good-bye and reminding his in-laws not to allow Joyce any contact with the kids without calling him first, Nick started the long boring ride back to Sunset Beach. Finding it almost impossible to concentrate between his worrying about Joyce's where-a-bouts, if she'll try to see the kids, and if his colleagues think he screwed up the Lee County investigation, he decided to ask Chief Thomas' help. He remembered that Chief told him that family always comes first.

Approaching DeeDee who was sitting at her desk, he asked her if he could have a few minutes of Chief's time promptly adding that is was a personal matter. DeeDee with a puzzled look on her face asked, "Didn't you see him at the Task Force meeting?"

Nick confused asked, "What Task Force meeting? No one told me about a meeting. I guess they all thought that I was still in Lee County."

Mumbling to himself that he'd better hustle his butt to the conference room, he hurried down the hall. Still thinking about not being told about this meeting, he literally bumped in to Chief Thomas who was exiting the Assistant Chief's office. Apologizing for not being on time for the meeting, Nick told the Chief that someone overlooked notifying him.

Appearing somewhat embarrassed Chief opened the door to the conference room where the meeting was in full swing. When the group realized that Nick had entered the room with the Chief, they fell silent. After a very uncomfortable few seconds Manny turned to the Chief and said, "Should I continue?"

Chief with that famous Cheshire cat smile said, "Might as well."

Looking Nick squarely in the eyes, Manny said, "As some of you know, I've just returned to Sunset Beach from Lee County and I'd like to bring you all up-to-date on the latest developments. I've obtained information about an on-going investigation regarding a woman living in the area, whose description," and turning to Nick said, "resembles your wife, Joyce.

Nick, placing his hands aggressively on the table, said, "Joyce? What the hell are you talking about? What has any of this got to do with Joyce?" He stared at Nick with a look that could kill.

Chief quickly interrupted and said, "Manny, I think we should continue this discussion in private. I'm going to adjourn this meeting for now. Why don't you all head back to your offices, finish whatever paper work needs completing, grab some lunch, and meet back here at one thirty."

Soundlessly the Task Force left the room. Nick and Manny walked back with Chief to his office. After closing the door,

Chief addressed Nick. With compassion in his voice, he said, "I hope you understand that we have no intention of embarrassing you in any way, nor do we doubt your dedication to the job. Though this is awkward for all of us, we have got to get to the bottom of some of these allegations."

Nick slumping into a chair just shook his head. Waiting until Nick got some control of his feelings, Manny said, "Let's start with the incident that happened here when Joyce came to visit you. To start with, you were really surprised to see her and also quite annoyed. I happened to be getting coffee when she began to ask you questions about the homicides. She also knew a lot of information that was never disclosed to the public. I didn't really start to get concerned until I mentioned it to Tina who told me that you have the reputation of never discussing a case you are working on with your family."

Nick, no longer being able to contain his anger said, "What is this bull shit? Look, Manny, you have had it in for me from the first day that we met, and I'm getting sick of your needling. So we missed the tire tracks at the scene. Don't tell me we are the only department that has ever overlooked a piece of evidence. And anyway, what has any of this got to do with Joyce?"

Chief, trying to keep the conversation civil, took over the questioning. "Look, Nick," he said. "when Joyce was here and met Officer Anderson who remarked that your wife was carrying a very unusual handbag. Do you know where she got it?"

Nick didn't care anymore that the man who just asked him this question was a Chief and answered, "Handbag? Handbag? How the hell should I know where she got it? Do you know where your wife buys her handbags? I think you're all crazy!"

Not wanting Nick to get any more agitated than he already was, Chief continued, "Look, we're asking these questions so that we can eliminate her as a suspect. It seems Grace Fields identified a handbag that she had bought her sister, victim Joan Simpson, and that it is now missing. Officer Anderson requested a catalog from the company so that we could not only have a description of the bag, but a picture as well. We expect it any day. I'm sure you understand why we have to check it out."

Nick angrily responded, "Now I know you're all crazy. How could Joyce be a suspect? Give me a motive. It certainly can't be jealousy. For God's sake, these women are old enough to be her mother!"

As soon as the statement left his mouth, Nick's entire body began to tremble. Stunned silent, he began thinking, "Her mother? Does she really hate her mother enough to kill anyone that even resembles her? Oh, my god ,Joyce, what have you done?"

Before Manny had a chance to bring up the investigation in Lee County, Nick grabbed his papers and stormed out of the room and said, "I can't listen to any more of this. I'm going home to my children..."

Reconvening the Task Force meeting at one-thirty, and before he let Manny bring them up to date, Chief, still steaming about having to get all his latest information from a bunch of civilians, let his staff know exactly how he felt. Not one to mince words, he told them that if they don't get their act together, there would be changes made, and that they wouldn't be happy. Continuing he added emphatically, "Not only can you all be replaced, but you can be replaced by three senior citizens who obviously know how to gather evidence a lot better than you can!"

Motioning to Manny to take over the meeting, he left to join Assistant Chief Kirk.

Chapter Twenty Four

Saturday, March 2nd

After speaking to Detective Arpell, TLTL were excited to be meeting with her again at eleven that morning. They were even more confident that they chose the right day and time because it was raining. It was Pam's suggestion to meet at eleven o'clock in the morning to knock on doors because, as she said, there are no doctor's appointments, bridge or golf lessons, committee meetings, Mah Jong or Canasta games scheduled. Laughing, Judy said that the only thing left to do on Saturday morning was for the ladies to have their hair done and the guys to play golf. Chiming in, Maxine said that they do that before ten. Since they arranged to meet Detective Arpell in the lobby at eleven, they checked their pockets to make sure they all have their *official police identification credentials* and off they go.

Detective Arpell who had arrived early seemed genuinely pleased to see the ladies as they exited the elevator. Quickly going over the strategy of the day, they were completely blown away when the detective produced a picture of a female suspect.(Unknown to TLTL, the department's experts had altered the picture by eliminating Nick's image from it.) They decided that one of TLTL will knock on the door and when the resident opens it up, they will introduce Detective Linda Arpell. Trying to be tactful and not wanting them to feel unimportant, Detective Arpell explained their role in the investigation.

"You Ladies are much more than window dressing. You play an important role in the scheme of things. We need your help and we're depending on you." Adding the *Mission Impossible* tag line, "Should you choose to accept this assignment," she cautioned, "instead of this conversation self-destructing, I will buy lunch."

With the biggest grins on their faces, TLTL assured her that she could count on them so..."Let's get started!"

Pretty much getting the same responses of "I don't know anything" or "I didn't see anyone" and feeling frustrated, Detective Arpell, who by this time TLTL were calling Linda, suggested that they do one more floor before they take a break.

Reaching Mrs. Zebrowski who had just gotten out of the shower, and who at least invited them in, reached for her glasses when handed the picture of Joyce and said, "Wait! I know her. She's the young lady that was with Beth the morning she died. I saw them together on the elevator. Now that I think about it, Beth never introduced me to her."

With this identification of the mystery lady and feeling energized, TLTL and Linda decided to continue. Reaching the Penthouse floor, it began to dawn on Judy that they were going to have to knock on Allan Grimm's door, and after what they had put him through, she secretly hoped he was not home.

Standing in front of his apartment Maxine said, "Oh, my God, this is Allan Grimm's apartment." Before she could suggest that they let Linda handle this on her own, Pam had already knocked.

Opening the door Allan Grimm's saw TLTL and his facial expression changed rapidly from cheerful to resentment. Starting to close the door in their faces, he stopped when he saw Detective Arpell. Getting angrier, if that was at all possible, he turned first to TLTL and said, "Haven't you busybodies done enough to disrupt my life?" Then lashing out to Detective Arpell he asked, "What could the Sunset Beach Police Department possibly want from me now?"

Pam began to apologize when Allan Grimm turned to Detective Arpell and demanded, "Tell me what you want and then all of you get out of my sight."

Detective Arpell quickly showed him the picture and was surprised to see his face soften. Answering her question if he had seen that woman in the building, he said, "No, but I have seen her somewhere. Let me think." Staring at the picture, he said, "Wait a minute. I remember. Her picture was in the Lee County Tribune. Something about a police gala and the man with her was her husband. I only remember it because my friend's picture was right next to hers."

Handing back the picture to the detective, he looked at the ladies out in the hallway and said, "Don't any one of you ever bother me again." He shut his door and locked it.

By getting two residents to identify Joyce, Arpell was ecstatic and reached for her cell phone to call Chief Thomas. Sharing the information they just uncovered, she told him that she was going to take the ladies out to lunch. Chief suggested that they chose a restaurant near the station and he would be honored to join them. Having lunch with the Chief was more than TLTL expected! Maxine chose the diner right across the street from the station. When Linda told the Chief about their choice of a restaurant and he answered, "Great. See you there in fifteen minutes."

After a pleasant and informative lunch, Chief thanked TLTL for all their help and leaned over to tell them that from now on he had a secret weapon for solving mysteries.

Looking somewhat confused, Detective Arpell asked, "And what could that be?"

Without any hesitation he said, "It's the ladies sitting right here. What would we have done without them?"

Chapter Twenty-Five

Monday, March 4th

After a very early morning meeting with Chief Thomas, Manny drove home to pack a few things and head back to Lee County. Traffic was extremely light on Alligator Alley and he was made excellent time. He began to think about Gladys Raphael and tried to figure out a way to meet her again. He stopped for breakfast in the town of Richmond where they met. Finding a small breakfast restaurant, he sat down in a booth and began to write an outline on what he needed to accomplish that day.

Engrossed in thought he was surprised to recognize a female voice saying, "Hey. Detective.....Are you lost again?" Looking up he was genuinely pleased to see Gladys.

Smiling he said, "You're not going to believe this, but I was just thinking about you."

Gladys boldly sat down opposite him and said, "You're right. I don't believe you," and began to laugh.

Manny promptly asked, "Would you care to join me for breakfast?"

Gladys replied, "I thought you'd never ask. If you're buying, I'm eating."

Like two old friends who hadn't seen each other for a while and wanted to catch up, they were busy chatting when suddenly looking at her watch Gladys said, "Oh, my God, I'm late for work. Jumping up and grabbing her purse, she said, "*Gotta go!*" She leaned across the table and kissed Manny on the cheek and said, "Thanks for breakfast."

Before she had a chance to run off, Manny took hold of her arm said, "Hey, lady, slow down. You just can't pop into my life, share mybreakfast and then kiss me off. I really was going to call you today and ask you to join me for dinner. The only two reasons I didn't call as soon as I arrived was, first I was hungry, so I stopped for breakfast; and second, I didn't know what the Sheriff has planned for me today or what time I'll be free. I thought when I knew what's on today's agenda, I would then give you a call. Where can I reach you between four and five?"

Handing him her card with her cell phone number written on the back she said, "You pick the time and I'll pick the place."

As she started to leave Manny said jokingly, "Try to pick a place that's easy to find. Remember, I'm a stranger in town and have no sense of direction."

Shaking her head she said, "See you later."

Not wanting to trigger the alarms in the Sheriff's Office again, Manny called ahead. Reaching Deputy Andrew Sultan, he arranged to meet him in the parking lot. When he arrived he saw the Deputy waiting in the sally port. Pointing out where he should park his car, Deputy Sultan waited and escorted him in to the building.

As they walked to his desk, Andrew told Manny that he had been up half the night re-reading the files on the two open homicides and still couldn't figure out where Joyce Russo fit in. "Try as I might, I can't find a link between Joyce and the victims, or for that matter, Nick and the victims. So, therefore, what is her motive? My head tells me that if there is no valid connection between them, we're barking up the wrong tree. My gut, however, keeps telling me that you're on to something. So I went through the files for the past two years and made a list of the names and addresses of anyone who witnessed or filed charges against a 30ish, white female that caused any kind of altercation on a senior citizen in a public place. I also made additional copies of Joyce's photo so that we can show it to them and see if anyone can identify her."

Reviewing the list he suggested they start with a Mr. & Mrs. Evan Laiken.Arriving in time to see Mr. Laiken stepping into his car, they quickly explained the reason for their visit. Mr. Laiken explained to them that his wife went to visit her sister and wouldn't be home until Friday. They then showed him Joyce's picture. Mr. Laiken straining to look at it said, "I can't be sure that this is the women that started the argument with my wife in Publix. We were both so upset. I'm sorry I can't be more of a help but I suffer with cataracts, and my vision is extremely poor." Closing the car door he proceeded to pull out of his driveway.

Andrew turned to Manny and laughing said, "Didn't he just tell us he can't see?"

Manny breaking out with a grin, said, "Yes, so how come you let him drive away? I thought we had all the bad drivers in South Florida, but it seems to me that you guys let anyone drive."

Still laughing Andrew said, "God help us."

Verifying the next name on the list, they drove to Mrs. Lona Shaler. Finding her in her kitchen they went through the same routine - showing their badges, explaining why they were there, and showing Joyce's picture. Just as Mr. Laiken couldn't identify the photo, neither could Mrs. Shaler.

After reaching out to four more people on the list and not finding them home, they left Deputy Sultan's card and decided to take a fast lunch break. Stopping at a local pizza place, Andrew saw Deputy Lori Hock and introduced her to Manny. Telling her a little about the similarity between their two open homicide cases and the two in Sunset Beach, he was careful about leaving out Nick's involvement.

They were immediately taken aback by what Deputy Hock told them next. She informed them that she recently ran into Nick Russo at the supermarket, and that he looked as though he was under a lot of stress. Lori said that she and Nick chatted a bit and when she told him that she had heard that he and Joyce decided to reconcile, he looked at her as if she lost her mind. Lori thought that Nick couldn't wait to get away from her.

"You know his twins and my Blake are in the same class and all the kids think that Joyce is a cool mother. Unlike me, she drives them to school everyday, never picks them up late and never punishes them when they get into fights, which must be all the time. I swear those kids always have black and blue marks somewhere on their bodies. Oh, speaking of picking up my kids on time I'd better get going."

After Deputy Hock left, Manny said to Andrew, "Black and blue? What did she mean that they are always black and blue? You can't tell me that Nick doesn't see that. What the hell is going on?"

Andrew with the anger beginning to show on his face said, "I don't know what the hell is happening in that house, but you can bet your ass I'm going to find out."

Driving in silence they arrived at Mandy and Jay Ritter's house.

As they approached the house, they heard the dogs barking and the TV blasting. Knocking on the door, they identified themselves as police officers as Mr. Ritter opened the door. Manny told him that they were investigating an incident that happened in Publix about a year and a half earlier. From the kitchen, Mandy Ritter's shouted, "It's about time! What took you so long?"

Joining her husband in the living room just in time to see Deputy Sultan show him the photo of Joyce, Mrs. Ritter said, "That's her. That's the women that started that ruckus. Don't you remember her? She was either drunk, on drugs or just plain crazy. I'll never forget her face."

Manny asked if they could walk them through the incident from the very beginning. Mrs. Ritter happily complied, "Jay and I were in the check out lane when we heard a commotion. This woman, the one in the picture, started screaming and cursing at this older woman who was putting her groceries on the counter next to us."

Interrupting, Detective Sultan asked, "What happened then? Could you hear what she was saying?"

Mandy Ritter, sounding a little annoyed, answered, "Everyone in the entire store could have heard her. Evidently the older woman must have bumped this younger women with her handbag while emptying her cart and the younger woman the one in your picture, began to yell 'hey lady, why don't you watch where you put your handbag. You just hit me with it.' After the older lady said she was sorry, and that she didn't realize she hit her, the younger women got this funny look on her face and shouted something like 'don't tell me your sorry, you're always sorry after you hit me with your handbag. One of these days I'm going to get even!' Really frightened, the older woman on the verge of hysterics, yelled, 'leave me alone or I'll call the police.'"

Jay Ritter interrupted his wife, "Didn't she shout go ahead and call the police; my husband is a deputy. See where it will get you."

Continuing Mandy Ritter said, "I don't know what would have happened if her children didn't start to cry and push her towards the door. The poor kids looked so scared. Come to think of it, they looked like twins. The store manager calmed the older lady down and suggested that she file a report with the Sheriff's office. I remember the lady saying, 'Are you crazy? You heard her. She said her husband is a deputy.'"

Thanking the Ritters for all their help, Andrew handed them his card and asked them to call him if they remembered anything else. Just before they reached the front door, Mr. Ritter stopped them, "Just a minute." Turning to his wife he said, "Weren't the Adams in the check out line behind us?"

"You know, I think your right," said Mrs. Ritter. "They must have heard what we heard. You ought to go to see them also. They live right around the corner."

Turning the corner they saw David Adams standing in the driveway obviously waiting for them to arrive. Introducing himself to Manny and Andrew, Mr. Adams told them that his wife, Irene, was on the phone with Mandy Ritter. Manny showed him Joyce's picture and he, too, identified Joyce as the lady in the store.

"I don't know if the Ritters told you but I heard her," and hesitating for a minute, looked at Andrew in his deputy uniform and said, "I hope you don't take offense at what I'm about to say, but the lady said that her husband was a Deputy Sheriff."

Trying to put Mr. Adams at ease, Andrew said, "No offense taken. I assure you that I'm going to give this information my full attention and personally check it out."

Heading back to the Sheriff's Department, both men were in deep thought and noticeably upset. Manny breaking the silence turned to Andrew and murmured, "Now we definitely know it's Joyce. We have all the pieces except the motive."

Interrupting, Andrew said, "We have a motive. She's fucking crazy. If you think the situation was bad before, wait until the press finds out the murderer may be a cop's wife. It's going to make this investigation a nightmare."

Manny nodding his head said, "For the Department's sake, I hope Nick is clean and that he didn't know what was going on. Hell, I don't know the guy all that well, but I really feel sorry for him. I'm glad I'm not the one who has to tell him."

As they continued to drive, Manny suddenly yelled, "Andrew stop! Quick, pull over. Am I seeing things, or is that Joyce Russo pulling into the U-Stor-It!?"

Finding a parking spot opposite the entrance to the building, Andrew said, "If that's not her, then she has a twin. Let's stay put until we can see where's she's headed. I don't want her to see a marked unit and get spooked. She must know by this time that Nick has reported her missing, and the last thing we need is a police pursuit if she decides to run."

Calling dispatch, Andrew requested an unmarked unit meet him at the U-Stor-It building. While giving them the address he saw Joyce begin to drive to the back of the storage bays area. Losing sight of her for less than a minute, they began to drive through the parking lot and realized that she managed to elude them by exiting from a back exit. Andrew, thoroughly disgusted, cancelled the back-up call and headed back to the Sheriff's office. As they entered the building, they saw Sheriff Wagner standing near Andrew's desk waiting for them. Recognizing the look on his face Andrew knew that he was in deep shit. He pointed to his office and both Andrew and Manny silently followed him in.

As soon as he closed the door, Sheriff Wagner turned and said, "How the hell could you lose her? Do you think she spotted you? Couldn't you have gotten any closer?" Not even waiting for an answer he continued, "Find out who owns U-Stor-It and contact them. Ask them to check their records to see if they rented a bay to a Joyce or Nick Russo. If they haven't, then have them check under the name of Joyce's parents. Get Joyce's license plate number. Most storage places keep a record of the cars that go in and out. I'm going to have a search warrant issued just in case we get lucky. Let's hope that the owners will be cooperative."

Looking at Manny, Sheriff Wagner told him that he would get in touch with Chief Thomas and bring him up-to-date, and suggested that he stick around for a while. As Sheriff Wagner picked up his phone, Andrew and Manny walked to Andrew's office and shut the door.

Andrew turned to Manny and said, "I don't think we screwed up. I think we made the right decision. If we had gotten any closer and she recognized me, then that would have also been my fault. Shit, I just can't win."

Manny, trying to smooth out the situation, said, "Chin up. You can always blame me. I'll be gone by tomorrow, unless my Chief calls and tells me to get my dumb ass back to Sunset Beach tonight." Just as he finished the sentence, his cell phone rang and the caller ID told him it was Chief Thomas.

Both men start to laugh as Manny picks up the phone. Without wasting any time, Chief asked, "What the hell is going on there? What did you do or didn't do?"

Manny answered, "Let me start from the beginning," and told the Chief exactly what happened.

Chief, listening intently, could feel a tightening in his stomach which is never a good sign. He asked Manny to see if Sheriff Wagner would be available about six-thirty this evening for a conference call and to get back to him when he had an answer.

Manny asked the Chief if he knew where Nick was and Chief answered, "No, I don't, but you can bet the farm that I'll find out. Do you think he's involved?"

Without hesitating Manny answered, "No."

Not relishing going back into the Sheriff's office, Manny opted to call him on the phone. Apologizing for disturbing him, he told him that Chief Thomas would like to know it he would be available for a conference call that evening at six-thirty. Answering that he would be, Sheriff Wagner added, "Oh by the way, please tell Andrew that if either you or he made plans for this evening, I strongly suggest you cancel them."

Giving Andrew the news about the evening he called Chief Thomas, and, not being able to reach him, told DeeDee that the conference call was all set. Deciding to call Gladys, Manny excused himself and told Andrew that he was going outside to make a phone call. Andrew, realizing that it must be personal, told him that he'd be knee-deep in paperwork and that he should take his time. Reaching Gladys, he told her that he was going to need a rain check for their dinner plans. He explained that they just uncovered some new evidence on the homicide case he was working on and that he had no idea what time he'd finish up.

Sounding disappointed Gladys answered, "It's okay; I understand."

About to say goodbye, Manny said, "Honestly, Gladys, I really want to see you. If I can get away before eleven, may I call you? Maybe we can meet for a cup of coffee?"

"I'd love it," she said. "Call me whenever you get through. I don't require a lot of sleep. I'm just naturally adorable"

Laughing Manny said, "Somehow from the minute I met you, I knew you were going to be trouble, and in a soft warm voice added, "Thanks for understanding."

Entering A/C Kirk's office, Mac brought him up-to-date on the latest developments and about the scheduled six-thirty conference call. Asking him to join him, he told him that he had decided not to include Tina in the conference call or to bring her up to speed. After all, she's an ME and not a cop, and he still was not sure of her relationship with Nick. Adding that, of course, Nick certainly wouldn't be told about what was going on until it was absolutely necessary.

Continuing on, the Chief told Jimmie, "I'm going to invite Sheriff Wagner to come down here tomorrow so that he can join us when we execute a warrant for Joyce's arrest. I'm also going to suggest that since he's Nick's boss, he should be the one to break the news to Nick before the press gets wind of what's going on."

Thoroughly concurring with all of Mac's decisions, Jimmie suggested that they also have their PIO Raychel Casper brought up to speed so that she can handle the press when all hell broke loose. Agreeing Mac asked him to please advise her and as he left, he said, "See you about six fifteen."

Promptly at six-thirty the phone rang in the Sheriff's office and turning on the video equipment he saw a razor sharp picture of Chief Thomas. After a cordial greeting, Chief

Thomas introduces A/C Jimmie Kirk, DeeDee, Detectives Arpell and Anderson, Sgt. Burns and PIO Raychel Casper.

In turn, Sheriff Wagner introduced his Under-Sheriff John Cabot, Deputies Andrew Sultan and Lori Hock. Smiling he said, "And of course, you do remember Detective Lopez."

As they began to go over all the evidence that was obtained in Lee County, especially the new information from the people that Manny and Deputy Sultan interviewed, Manny said "I have no doubt that Joyce Russo is not only a murderer, but is also mentally unbalanced. She is a danger to the herself, her family, and the community. The most disturbing piece missing to this puzzle is that no one knows where the hell she is and that she needs to be taken off the streets immediately."

Deputy Sultan started to relate the afternoon's incident about seeing Joyce at a storage facility when Sheriff Wagner interjected that he had already started the ball rolling. He related that he had reached the owners of U-Stor-It Company who had agreed to cooperate.He told them that he had already had a deputy return to the storage office where the bookkeeper identified Joyce's picture. Obtaining her bin number, he contacted Judge Holmes for a search warrant and as soon as she signed the warrant, they would begin to initiate a search.

As the conference call started to wind down, Chief Thomas invited Sheriff Wagner to attend the press conference that they were going to schedule for the following afternoon. He expressed his appreciation for all the help he and his department extended to him, and that he also believed it was important that the public knew that this was a joint effort. The Chief and the Sheriff agreed that if they were pressed by the media for specifics, they would refer to Joyce Russo as a person of interest. Sheriff Wagner accepted Chief's invitation to join him at his press conference. Chief then asked him if he could be the one to tell Nick what was taking place before the news media broke the story. Sheriff Wagner assured Chief that he would be in Sunset Beach around noon and suggested that they tell Nick together. Ending the conference call, and agreeing to keep each in the loop, Chief Thomas disconnected the video and sound.

Manny, checking his watch, was happy to see that it was only seven forty-five. Reaching for his cell phone, he called Gladys.

Recognizing the number, Gladys picked up on the first ring. Manny told her that he had just finished with his conference call, and although the Chief wanted him back at the office by eight in the morning, he hoped that they could still have dinner together.

Gladys told him about a café right near the Sheriff's office where they could catch a light bite and guaranteed him that it would be impossible for him to get lost. She asked, "Are you calling from the parking lot of the Sheriff's Office?

When Manny told her that he was, Gladys replied, "Okay, if you are facing the building, turn around and face north. Do you see a store front at the end of the street?"

He answered, "Yep." She told Manny to start walking that way and he'd see the sign that said *"Blue Bay Café"*.

"When you get there, grab a table for two and I'll join you in less than ten minutes."

As he walked to the restaurant, Manny's cell started to ring. Checking the number, he was surprised to see that it was A/C Kirk who told him that there was some information that Chief didn't want to discuss with everyone in the room, but, wanted him to know before they met in the morning.

His curiosity was aroused when Kirk told him that they had deliberately left Tina out of the meeting. He asked him to see if he could get information on whether or not Tina and Nick were or are an item and to call either him or the Chief back if he heard anything. Telling A/C that he'd call Deputy Sultan and call him back either way, he made a point to let him know that he was going to stop for a bite before he started home.

By the time the call ended, Manny had reached the restaurant, and after being shown to a table, he called Andrew Sultan. Andrew sounded a little surprised to hear from Manny so soon and said, "Do you miss me already? Or are you lost?"

Answering neither, Manny told Andrew the reason for the call. Asking if he had ever heard talk of a relationship other than work between Nick Russo and Tina Lange when she worked in Lee County, Andrew without delay said, "No, I remember that Tina was involved with someone she met in Medical School, but it didn't work out. Anyway Nick and Tina rarely had occasion to work together, so again I'd have to say no."

Thanking him, Nick saw the door to the restaurant open and Gladys walk in. Thinking to himself that yep, she's right. She is adorable. He stood as she reached the table.

"Who said chivalry is dead?" Gladys greeted him and kissed him on the check and sat down. The dinner conversation was easy and relaxing with neither one of them feeling any pressure to put on an act. They were both happy to be getting to know each other. Realizing that the evening was coming to an end when the coffee was served, and not knowing if they would see each other again, the mood became somber.

Manny, not being able to contain his feelings said, "Do you know, Gladys, that you are a very special lady? And one that I would really like to get to know better?"

Gladys for the first time sounding almost shy said, "I'd also like to get to know you better. I won't hide how disappointed I am that you have to return home tonight. It isn't that I didn't know that you were going to go home sooner or later. I guess I was hoping for later much later than tonight. Let's just lie to each other and promise that we'll keep in touch and meet each other half way for lunch at least once a month. So now all that is left is for you to get up, pay the check and walk me to my car and end this evening with a friendly hug and kiss."

Upon reaching her car, Manny gently pulled Gladys to him. Taking her in his arms, he slowly began to kiss her and she began to respond with the same intensity.

After several minutes Gladys said, "Listen, we'd better stop this before the headline in tomorrow's paper reads *Sunset Beach Detective and Richmond Police Department's receptionist arrested for indecent behavior in the parking lot of a local family restaurant.*"

"Yeah, you're right, but you feel so good. I don't ever want to stop holding you. Ah, what the hell, let's just get arrested."

Laughing Gladys puts both her hands on Manny's chest and pushes him back just far enough to be able to get into her car. Starting her car and running her window down, Gladys accepted Manny's lingering kiss. Standing up, he said, "I promise I will call you!"

Chapter Twenty-Six
Tuesday, March 5th

Arriving at the station, Manny walked straight into Chief Thomas' office. Finding everyone already there and skipping the preliminaries, Chief asked, "Did you bring the picture of Joyce Russo?"

"Yes, sir. It's right here." Reaching into his briefcase he pulled out the snapshot. DeeDee offered to make enough copies for road patrol and to have them distributed to all three shifts.

Chief then continued, "I want road patrol to stop at every supermarket, drug store, and restaurant in their zones - not only to show Joyce's picture to the employees, but to speak to every store manager personally.

Detective Arpell volunteered to help the record clerks go back at least one year to see if anyone reported any similar incidents in either the local supermarkets or discount stores.

Manny reminded Chief that Sheriff Wagner would be there about noon. Chief told him to keep himself available and asked him if had gotten the information he requested from Lee County.

Manny realizing that Chief did not want to discuss it in front of the Task Force answered, "Yes, and there is no validity to it." Smiling at his diplomacy Chief nodded his head in approval.

Road Patrol Officer Richard Gibbons called Chief very excitedly talking a mile a minute. Mac said, "Hey, Rich, slow down. I can barely understand a thing you're saying."

"Sorry sir. I'm at the *All U Can Eat Ribs* joint on US 1 and Pembroke Road, and the manager, Bradley Firman, recognized the woman in the picture. He's telling me that the woman in the photo had a fight with an older lady back in early January. He said that the ruckus started because the older woman accidentally brushed up against her with her handbag while they were waiting to be seated. She went absolutely ape-shit... screaming and cursing...claiming that the older woman was trying to kill her. He said he had to ask the younger woman to leave, and after cursing at him, she turned to the older woman and screamed, 'I promise you'll regret this bitch.'"

Gibbons told Chief that the manager remembered the incident like it was yesterday. He comped the older woman's meal as he didn't want to lose her as a customer. Chief asked Gibbons if the manager could come into the station for a formal statement and look at some other photos. When Gibbons came back on the line, he told Chief that Mr. Firman would be there in about fifteen minutes but his time was limited since he would need to be back at his restaurant by eleven fifteen to supervisor the lunch hour. Promising that he would have him back in time, even if he had to personally drive him, Chief hung up.

Chief buzzed DeeDee and asked her to contact Detectives Arpell and Anderson and have them meet him in the conference room in fifteen minutes. Before he could catch his breath, his direct line began to ring. Answering, he heard a woman's voice and was almost speechless when he recognized it as Francine Bolton. Trying to regain his composure he began to make small talk. Francine, wanting no part of that, got right to the point.

She told him that she was calling from Quantico with Agent Bob Rogers who was the leading profiler for the FBI. Without waiting for a comment, she continued saying that they thought they had come up with some helpful information on his homicides.

His interest perked, Chief said, "Go on."

"Well, the evidence we submitted for analysis through our national computer tracking system, reveals that there is a strong possibility that our serial killer is a woman. Notice I said *serial killer*. They are certain that the same person committed all four homicides. The profiler believes that the murderer is in her late thirties. From the angle of the force applied to the victims' necks she's approximately five feet three inches tall and weighs between 135 and 140 pounds."

Chief thanked her profusely for all her help and Francine informed him that she was going to fax him all the information. Before Chief had a chance to say anything on a personal level, she hung up.

DeeDee announced the arrival of Bradley Firman, and after the introductions, both he and Chief walked to the conference room. Finding both Detectives already seated, they showed Mr. Firman a photo line-up. He immediately pointed to Joan Simpson and identified her as the customer that was threatened.

Trying to restrain his enthusiasm, Chief whispered to Detective Arpell, "Yes! We got her! Finally we have a connection between Joyce and our victim, Joan Simpson."

After receiving Chief's promise to have him back at his restaurant before eleven, Mr. Firman agreed to give a written statement describing the incident. Mr. Firman turned to Detective Anderson and smiling said, "Let's get started."

Almost like magic, the stress began to leave Chief's face as he headed back to his office.

Sheriff Wagner pulled into the Sunset Beach Police Department exactly at noon. DeeDee, seeing him arrive on the closed circuit T.V. installed on her desk, got up to greet him and escort him into the Chief's office.

After the usual handshake, Chief turned to the Sheriff and said, "Damn it, Dan, how are we going to handle this mess? I feel as though I aged 20 years." The Sheriff shook his head from side to side. "Some times I really hate my job; and today is one of them."

Mac gave him a brief overview on what had taken place in the last two days. He showed him the statement that Mr. Firman had just signed pointing out the paragraph which described his recognition of Joyce Russo as the woman who verbally assaulted one of his customers, Joan Simpson. Mac told Dan that Joan Simpson was their first victim.

Realizing that they can no longer ignore the Nick Russo problem, Mac asked Dan how he wanted to handle it. Dan answered, "Truthfully, Mac, I just don't know. And I'm certainly open to suggestions."

Mac, sitting silently for a moment, said, "There is no easy solution. I guess we just have to bite the bullet. Let's just get him on the phone and bring him in." Agreeing, Dan reached for his phone and dialed Nick.

Nick, somewhat surprised to see the Sheriff's number come up on his caller ID, immediately answered it. Sheriff Wagner informed Nick that he was in town and would like to meet with him. He told him that he would be at the Sunset Beach Police Department at two and was ,looking forward to seeing him there. Before Nick could ask any questions, the line went dead.

Nick, confused and unnerved, thought to himself, "This can't be good; I must have really stepped in it big time."

After hanging up, Dan turned to Mac and said, "That was the easy part. Talking to him in person is going to be tough."

Mac agreed with him and said, "Let's discuss how you're going to handle it." Offering his office for privacy, Mac said, "Dan, I could leave and let the two of you talk this out or I could hang around just for support. However you decide to handle it will be alright with me."

Dan asked Mac to stay and he began to write a list of what needed to be said:
 a) Show Nick all the evidence including the statement from Mr. Firman.
 b) Tell him about the storage rental in Joyce's name.
 c) Offer complete support to both him and his family.
 d) Suggest he call his in-laws to let them know what's happening so they can take the steps to protect the children from the press.

All that is left to do is now is to grab some lunch and wait for Nick.

For the past agonizing hour, Nick had been pacing the floor and watching the clock. Trying to reach Tina he was told that she was in the middle of an autopsy and would not be available until about four o'clock.He called his in-law's house to see how the twins were, and he reached the Nanny.

Telling him that the children were in school and that his in-laws are out food shopping, she asked if he wanted to leave a message. Nick answered that he would call back and was surprised when, out of the blue, the Nanny asked if everything was alright.

Nick answered, "Of course, why?"

"Forgive me if I have overstepped my bounds," said the Nanny, "but your voice sounds so stressed."

Nick, not wanting to make an issue out of an innocent question, told her that he was pre-occupied with the case he was working on and thanked her for her concern. Hanging up, he began to think, if I sound this stressed over the phone to our Nanny, imagine what I will sound like when I meet the Sheriff in person. I have got to get my act together.

Nick arrived a few minutes before two and upon entering the building saw DeeDee approaching him. She offered to accompany him to Chief's office. He tried to control the shaking of his hands.

Seeing both the Sheriff and the Chief sitting in the small conference room adjacent to the Chief's office didn't do anything to ease his feeling of impending doom that was rapidly taking over. Showing him to a seat, Sheriff Wagner wasted no time telling him why he was there. Not mincing words, he lay out all the evidence that both departments had collected.

"Look Nick, you're a cop. I'm not going to insult your intelligence by sugar-coating the facts. Just by looking over the statement from the manager of the restaurant you have to realize that this is serious and that it doesn't look good."

Feeling as though someone has just punched him in the stomach Nick was finding it difficult to breathe. All he could say over and over was, "Oh, my God. Oh, my God, this can't be happening." As he rocked back and forth he began to chant, "Joyce, what have you done? What have you done?" Looking directly at the Sheriff, Nick said, "Sir, you know my wife. You've had dinner at our house. How could you believe Joyce capable of such a thing?"

Trying to calm him down, the Sheriff said, "Nick, I didn't want to believe it either, but I can't deny the evidence. And, Nick, neither will you. Right now, you have to let us do our job and you have to concentrate on your twins. They're going to need a father that will be strong and available. I promise you that I will have someone keep you in the loop and will send out the word to handle Joyce as gently as she will allow."

Chief Thomas interrupted and told Nick that the next few hours will not only have an impact on him, but on his family as well. Once the press got wind of this there would be no stopping them. Nick put his face in his hands and began to sob.

The sound of Sheriff Wagner's cell phone ringing seemed to bring Nick back in focus. The Sheriff told Mac that it was his deputy, Andrew Sultan, with information on the search warrant that was served about a half hour ago. Hearing the words *search warrant,* Nick sat straight up. Putting the call on speaker phone, Sheriff Wagner told Andrew that he was now on speaker and that Chief Thomas and Nick Russo were also in the room. He asked, "You sure you want me to discuss the results of the search warrant and the contents found in the storage locker?"

Sheriff said, "Yes, go ahead. Nick is aware of what is going on."

Forging ahead Andrew said, "They opened the locker and found two barrels. The first one contained a bunch of junk... broken toys, old clothing, and picture albums. The second barrel contained ladies shoes, pink blankets and scarves. But right behind the barrels they discovered an old chest of drawers containing handbags. Some looked as though they were there for a long time, kinda moldy smelling. Then there were four bags wrapped in tissue and then put in individual plastic bags as though to preserve them. I sent the bags to the lab to see if we could get prints off the plastic."

Stopping almost in the middle of a sentence he told Nick how sorry he was to have to do this, but getting no response from him continued. "I had one of the deputies check the data base in the computer and it confirmed that Joyce Russo's prints are on are file. Before the twins were born, Joyce worked as a healthcare provider in one of the assisted living facilities in Lee County. As you're aware, fingerprinting the personnel is mandatory. I'm sure if there are readable prints on the bags, it will be easy for us to run a fingerprints check." Andrew also told them that the blankets they found were tested and were from the same dye lot of those in their evidence locker.

Nick, not being able to contain himself any longer, got up and walked to the door. Turning to the Sheriff he mumbled, "I'm having trouble breathing. I need to get some air." Seeing the look on Chief Thomas' face Nick added, "Don't worry, Chief, I won't take off. I don't have any place to go."

Chief decided to call a Task Force meeting for four pm and invited the Sheriff to join him. Exactly at four, Assistant Chief Kirk arrived followed by Sgt. Burns, Detectives Arpell, Anderson, and Lopez. Introducing Sheriff Wagner and before speculation could begin, Chief said, "Let's get started."

Sgt. Burns turned and whispered to Detective Arpell, "Aren't we going to wait for Nick and Tina?"

Overhearing their conversation, Chief answered harshly, "No."

A Murder 2 Die 4

Without further delay, Chief dropped the bombshell, "Sit back in your chairs, listen to what I have to say, and when I'm through, either Sheriff Wagner or myself will answer all of your questions. I have just received the evidence needed to make an arrest on all four homicide cases."

Taking a deep breath and turning to the group Chief said, "Our suspect is ....Joyce Russo. Nick's wife." The old saying that *the sound of silence can be deadly* could not be truer than at this very moment. You could hear a pin drop. "Sheriff Wagner and I have already spoken with Nick and he's trying to cope. I know I can count on all of you to offer the support that he and his family will need. Look, things are going to start happening very quickly. We need to get our ducks in order before the press gets wind of this. The local media will be all over us when we announce that we have a suspect in custody. When they realize that it's a serial killer, they will be relentless. Also, once they find out that our suspect is not only a woman, but the wife of a police officer, we're talking national news. Trust me when I say life in our small town and in Lee County will never be the same. If for any reason the press picks up on this tonight, remember that we are not calling Joyce Russo a suspect at this time. She is, however, *a person of interest*. Let me suggest that you all try to get a good night's sleep and plan to meet back here tomorrow after roll call."

Sheriff Wagner, thanking everyone for their help, told them that they were going to try to keep Nick Russo under the radar. They would be checking him out of his motel and taking him to stay with a friend at least for tonight. Nick was planning to attend tomorrow's Task Force meeting and then would be returning to Lee County.

Chief asked if there were any questions and getting no reaction turned and left the room with Sheriff Wagner. On their way back to Mac's office, Dan Wagner asked him, "What are we going to do with Nick? I can't even imagine what he's going through. If he doesn't have anyone that he can stay with, I am going to insist that he stay with me at my cousin's home as I don't want him to spend the evening alone."

Returning to his office, Mac saw Nick on his cell phone with his back to the door. Chief overheard him say that if he ever needed a friend he needed one now. Nick, still oblivious that anyone had entered the room, continued. "I'm going to check out of my motel because Joyce knows where I'm staying. I'll throw my things together and then I'll pick up dinner." Nick humbly said, "Thanks again, Tina. I don't know what I would do without you."

Hanging up he turned around and saw both the Sheriff and the Chief standing in the doorway. Not wanting to ask how long they had been there, or what they had heard, he simply said, "I'm going to be staying at Tina Lange's tonight."

Trying to ease the awkwardness of the moment Sheriff Wagner told him that he would call him in the morning. Nick nodded and walked out the door. Mac invited Dan to join him for dinner, but he declined telling him that he had relatives in Pembroke Pines and would see him in the morning.

Finding himself alone for the first time all day, Chief picked up his phone and called his wife Ellen. In a voice that echoed the stress of the day, he just said, "Honey, I'm on my way home."

After spending the afternoon shopping and stopping for dinner, TLTL returned home. Entering the lobby of their condo, Maxine turned to Pam and Judy and suggested that they stop off at Beth's apartment before going on to their own. Looking somewhat puzzled, Pam asked why. Maxine reminded her that the last time they were in Beth's apartment, they never threw out the trash in her recycling bin and that the following day was a scheduled pick-up day.

Agreeing, Pam dug into her purse and produced Beth's keys. As they entered the apartment and walked to the kitchen, the emptiness became apparent. Judy, her eyes filling with tears, said, "Let's do this quickly. I just can't stand being here without Beth."

Heading straight for the area that Beth kept her bin, Maxine saw an empty bottle of Starbuck's Mocha Frappuccino lying right on top of the bin. Wrinkling her brow and pointing to it, she turned to Pam. "This is strange. Why would Beth have a bottle of coffee in her garbage? In all the years we knew her, did you ever see her drink coffee?"

Pam replied, "No, you know she always said that it gave her heart burn."

"Okay," said Maxine, "then what the hell is this bottle doing here?" Before anyone can reach for the bottle Maxine said, "Girls, don't touch that bottle. I know you're going to laugh at me when I tell you that last night on *CSI Miami*, the episode was all about the CSI detectives finding an empty bottle of Scotch in the trash. The wife insisted that it wasn't theirs because they only drank Vodka. Because the detectives were able to obtain fingerprints from the bottle, they were able to solve the crime and correctly identify the killer to arrest him."

Judy, getting very antsy said, "Don't not touch anything. Maxine could be right. This is just too much for my nerves. Let's just close the door and call Chief Thomas from the lobby."

Checking her watch Pam said, "It's after six. I'm sure that the Chief has left for the day."

Maxine butted in, "I'm going to call anyway. If he's not there, then I'll just leave a message."

Calling the SBPD, she reached dispatch who told her that the Chief left for the day and asked if she would like to leave a message. Not wanting to sound like a panic-stricken resident, she said to have him call her, adding that it was really important. The dispatcher tagged it as a non-emergency call and simply put it in Chief's box.

After another sleepless night, Chief Thomas arrived at the Sunset Beach Police Department. Deep in thought he heard the dispatcher call his name. As she approached him she handed him the message she retrieved from his box and said, "This call came in last night."

Reading the message, he became enraged. Turning to her, he asked, "Who took this message?"

DeeDee, who had just entered the building, hurried to where the Chief was standing and tried to defuse what was beginning to look like something that may escalate into an extremely unpleasant incident. She asked, "Is there anything I can do?"

Showing her the message he was just handed, he told her, "Yeah, find out who is now making the decisions on what is priority for this Department and also for me! But before you do, get me Maxine Greene!"

As he slammed the door to his office, DeeDee shook her head and decided to let him cool off for awhile and handle the dispatcher herself.

Maxine was sitting in her kitchen and staring into space when her phone rang. Checking her caller ID and seeing that the number was blocked, she hesitated to answer it, but decided to pick it up anyway. Hearing DeeDee say, "Please hold for Chief Mac", Maxine suddenly felt drained.

Chief started the conversation off by apologizing for not returning her phone call until today. Without wasting time, Maxine related the incident that prompted it. Totally in awe of these ladies, Chief informed Maxine that he would dispatch a unit to her apartment to pick up the bottle and the contents of the recycling bin - just in case there was anything else that may be evidence.

Maxine offered to bring them to him saying, "I know how busy you are and the carton is very light. Trust me, you need not worry about our tampering with the evidence. The girls and I know better." With a youthful giggle she said, "We learned from *CSI Miami*."

Chief, unable to contain his laughter, said, "Maxine, I don't know what I'd do without you. This just could be the part of the puzzle that we're missing. It could be the one piece that could nail the killer."

Sounding as excited as if she had just won the lottery, Maxine told him that she would be there within the hour. She then called Judy and Pam. After relating her conversation with the Chief, she told the girls to throw on some clothes, forget the make-up, and meet her in the lobby in a half hour.

DeeDee knocked on Chief's door to let him know that Sheriff Wagner had just pulled into the parking lot and was on his way into the building. After bringing him into the Chief's office, DeeDee closed the door behind her.

Settling in his chair, Chief told the Sheriff about his secret squad of investigators that he calls *The Ladies That Lunch*.

Looking somewhat amused and confused, Sheriff Wagner, smiling, asked, "Would you like to elaborate?"

Mac, smiling quickly, said, "Nope. Just be patient. You'll get the opportunity to meet them in person. They are on their way over."

While discussing Nick and the fallout of Joyce's arrest on both departments, they heard loud voices in the hall. Getting up and opening the door, they saw TLTL carrying a box and refusing to let anyone take it from them. DeeDee, walking towards them, told everyone else to back off. Winking at the two officers who were trying to help she said, "These ladies are on special assignment and are working directly with the Chief."

Sheriff Wagner grinning said, "So these are your secret weapon?" Mac answered yes to the sheriff and to TLTL said, "Ladies, I'd like you to meet Sheriff Wagner. He's from the Lee County Sheriff's Office.

After acknowledging the Sheriff's presence, the ladies got right to the point. Maxine handed him the recycling bin and told him that Beth did not drink coffee so there was no reason for a Starbucks bottle to be in her apartment.

Buzzing for DeeDee, Chief asked her to contact Sgt. Burns ASAP. And feeling it necessary, explained to the ladies that he was their fingerprint expert.

Standing up Maxine turned to the girls and said, "Let's go, ladies. These men have work to do!"

Chief Thomas, walking around his desk, kissed each one of TLTL on the check and escorted them to the door. Smiling at Maxine, he said, "I may make it a requirement for each of my officers to watch *CSI Miami* before they can get re-certified," and thanking her once again, gave her a hug.

After TLTL left, Sheriff Wagner jokingly said to Mac, "I can't believe what just took place. You mean to tell me that these senior citizens may have single-handedly solved four homicides that two professional law enforcement agencies couldn't do? If this ever gets out, we both better retire, because we'll never live it down."

Mac looking at Dan with a wicked grin said, "Wait, there's more. These ladies were also responsible for getting the first three letters of Joyce Russo's license plate."

Sgt. Burns knocked on the door and entered the office. Chief handed him the recycling bin TLTL brought in and explained the significance of the Starbuck's bottle. Carrying the bin, Sgt. Burns said, "I'll get on it right away and will call you as soon as I get any results."

As he left, Sheriff Wagner suggested that they call Nick and have both him and Tina attend the Task Force meeting.

Nick arrived at Tina's apartment. During dinner Nick updated Tina about the evidence that pointed to Joyce. The next morning after Tina awoke, she headed quietly to the kitchen in order not to disturb Nick. While making coffee she heard Nick softly call her name.

"I'm in the kitchen, sleepy head."

Hearing no response Tina started to return to her bedroom when she saw Nick standing in the foyer. Holding up an envelope he said, "Look what I found slipped under your door. Do you have anything I can use to open the envelope without disturbing any fingerprints that might be on it?"

"Just a minute," and she returned with a pair of surgical gloves.

Slipping his hands into the gloves, Nick opened the envelope. Watching his facial expression change as he read the note, Tina nervously asked, "What's wrong? Tell me, what does it say?"

He hesitated then read aloud:
SLUT....YOU'RE NEXT

As Nick reached to comfort Tina his cell phone rang. Thinking it might be Sheriff Wagner, he answered it immediately. The Sheriff started off by asking Nick how he was doing and Nick answered that he was hanging in there. Telling him of the scheduled Task Force meeting set for nine o'clock that morning, he reminded him that he had asked to be included. The Sheriff then asked if Tina was there. Replying that she was, Sheriff Wagner asked Nick to please let her know that Chief Thomas also expected her to attend. Nick told him that they both would be there in thirty minutes.

Hanging up he turned to Tina and said, "We both need to be at your station in thirty minutes. I guess we better get a move on. We'll have to figure out how to handle this note after the meeting."

Grabbing the duffle bag that he brought from the motel, he pulled out a pair of jeans and a tee shirt, and, while putting them on, told Tina that while she was getting dressed, he was going to stop off at an ATM, fill up his car with gas, and then come back and pick her up. Tina told him to go on ahead and she'd meet him at the station. But, Nick not wanting to leave her alone in her apartment, told her that he'd wait for her to get ready before he did the few errands.

Tina shaking her head said, "Listen, Nick, that's ridiculous. I'm perfectly capable of driving my own car."

Promising to be careful and to leave in just a few minutes, she kissed him on the cheek, gently pushed him out the door and locking it, returned to her bedroom to dress and put the finishing touches on her make-up. Finally ready to leave, she unlocked her door and, as she opened it, she was shoved backwards and heard a woman's voice saying, *"Where do you think you're going, slut?"*

When Nick entered the conference room, he found the Task Force meeting already engaged in deep conversation. There was an uncomfortable silence as the group saw him. Finally Captain Anderson told him how sorry she was for the situation that he and his family would be facing. She assured him that if there was anything he needed them to do to help him, all he had to do was ask.

Before Nick had a chance to respond, Sgt. Burns entered the room. Apologizing for interrupting, he turned to the Chief and said, "I have the preliminary report of the fingerprints that were found on the bottle of Starbucks coffee and they are a fifteen point match."

Suddenly, Nick jumped up, scanned the room and with urgency in his voice shouted, "*Where's Tina?!*"

Not getting a reaction, Nick said, "She should have been here ten minutes ago. *Oh My God!* What have I done? I never should have left her alone. Not after that note."

Chief Thomas trying to calm him down asked, "What the hell is going on? Why are you so worried about Tina running a little late? And what's this about a note?"

Repeating, "*Oh My God*", Nick told the Chief about the threatening note slipped under Tina's door. Almost out of control, Nick shouted, "We have to dispatch a unit to Tina's house now. If what you are telling me about Joyce is true, Tina is in grave danger."

Trying to reach her first on her on her cell and receiving no answer, Nick tried her home number. Receiving a busy signal Nick began to panic. Chief Thomas immediately dialed 911. Asking Nick for Tina's address, he then identified himself and instructed the emergency dispatcher to send a unit to 10120 Adams Street in Hollywood Bay and requested a *Code One* (no lights or sirens) when responding. He also advised them that the Sunset Beach Police Department was also responding.

The Chief then dialed the Hollywood Bay Police Department and asked for Chief Dick Fox. His secretary Sonya recognized his voice and put him through immediately.

Hearing Chief Fox's voice, Chief Thomas told him, "Dick, I need your help. Our ME may be in trouble. There's a possibility that our suspect in the beach homicides is either on her way to Tina's apartment or is already there. I've call 9-1-1 and asked them to dispatch a unit, and, hopefully, they're on their way now."

"I've already been notified, Mac, and I'm on the way to Tina's. Let's talk more when we get there. Is there anything else I can handle before I leave?"

"I don't think so, Dick. I issued an APB on a late model Dodge Durango with the first three letters on the Florida tag Juliet Sierra Romeo. The suspect is Joyce Russo. White female, age 35, approximately 5 feet 3 inches, 135 pounds. She has short blonde hair and brown eyes, and, Dick, she's a signal 20. (mentally ill) Tell your guys to proceed with caution. Just between us, her husband is on the job with LCSO. We're on our way, and I'm bringing the husband with me. Hopefully he can help before anyone else gets hurt."

While Chief Thomas was dialing Chief Fox, Manny told Nick that he'd get his car and meet him out back. Reaching the first floor, the group is bombarded with cameras rolling and questions being asked from the press who have all gathered in the lobby. Ignoring the media they bolted out the back door as Manny pulled the car around for the Chief and Sheriff.

Once inside Nick dialed Tina again. Still getting no answer, Nick decided to try Joyce's cell. Getting her voice message, Nick turned to Manny and said, "You'd better step on it. All my instincts are telling me that Tina is in grave danger. I only hope we're not too late."

Looking through the rear view mirror, Manny saw the local WSBN news van following right behind them. Asking Chief if he should try to lose it, Chief just shook his head in disgust and said, "Why bother? I'm sure their helicopters will be over the building the minute they get a fix on where we're headed."

Nick now talking to Sheriff Wagner said, "The press is going to have a field day with this. I can just see the lead in for the afternoon news: *Cop's wife accused in the Golden Girls murders... Film at five."*

He began to worry, "What will happen to my kids? How are they going to handle the pressure not only from the press but from their peers? What if I'm accused of a cover up? Oh my God, what am I going to do?"

Sheriff Wagner, concerned that Nick was totally out of control, tried to reason with him. "Nick, get a grip on things. If you don't, you won't be of any help to anyone." As he reminded him that too many people needed to be able to count on him - such as his twins for one and the department for another - Manny pulled into the parking lot right behind the Hollywood Bay Police Department's vehicles. As they exited the car, the Chief, the Sheriff and Nick were met by Chief Fox. Looking around the parking lot Nick spied Joyce's black Durango and was now certain that Joyce was definitely the murderer and silently prayed for Tina's safety.

Bringing everyone current, Chief Fox told them that the neighbors on Tina's floor have all been alerted and were in the process of being escorted out of the building. All units and personnel were being told to park their vehicles behind the east side of the building. They also set up an area for the media.

"We've made this decision because the windows in Tina's apartment all face east, and if Joyce looks out the window, she won't see any police units. Hopefully, it may make her think she is safe and not do anything stupid."

Now focusing on Nick, Chief Fox's asked, "Do you think if we allow you to join the negotiating team, you will be able to talk to your wife or do you think if she hears your voice, you will make matters worse?"

Without waiting for an answer Chief Fox continued, "Provided, of course, that she hasn't already harmed Tina?"

Nick quickly answered, "Yes, I'm sure I can reach her."

Chief Fox, cutting him short, said, "Keep in mind that she is irrational. She also thinks that the woman inside has been having an affair with you. Not only is she capable of hurting Tina, but you as well.

"Please," Nick responded, "at least let me try. Just give me a few minutes with her. I don't want anyone else hurt. If I see that I'm not helping, I promise to step back and let your team take over."

"If I agree, I want you to know that at anytime I feel that you are not in total control, we will take over immediately. And you *will* wear a vest. Is that clear?"

Not wanting to jeopardize the chance to end this peaceably, Nick agreed. Putting on his vest, he entered the building with the SWAT team close behind. Reaching Tina's door, he tried the handle and was surprised that the door was unlocked.

Opening the door slowly he said, "Joyce, it's Nick. I'm coming in and I'm alone. I just want to talk to you." He motioned to the officers that are behind him to step to the side so they wouldn't be seen.

As the door fully opened, he spotted Tina in the hallway with Joyce directly behind her. Sizing up the situation, he saw that Joyce had one arm across Tina's neck and her other hand along the side of her head. Nick realized that Joyce could easily snap Tina's neck from that position and all three of them knew it. Walking slowly into the apartment, Nick was banking on the fact that if he kept Joyce talking, he may be able to get her to release Tina or at least get close enough to neutralize the attack.

Starting a dialogue, he said, "Joyce, honey, don't take out our problems on Tina. They're not her fault. I'm the one who walked out. I'm the one who's neglected you. I'm the one who is always too busy working to help the twins. Please, Joyce, let's talk this out. I'm really so sorry. I know we can work things out. I promise to make time for you. I'm really willing to change."

Joyce, completely out of control, began to shout, "Sure, now you want to talk. I know why you didn't come home. You were having an affair with this slut."

Nick, trying to keep his voice on an even keel, was careful not to say anything that would agitate her even more. He pled, "What can I say? What can I do to make you believe that I love you? I worked all those hours so that you and the twins will have a good life. I was wrong. I never realized how much I neglected you. Please, Joyce, I know we can work this out together. Let me help you. Just let Tina go."

As Joyce doubled over gasping for air, Nick grabbed Tina and shoved her out the door and into the arms of one of the Hollywood Bay officers. In a matter of seconds the stand off is over. Before Joyce could straighten up or realize what had happened, the SWAT team entered the apartment. Nick shouted, "Guys! Please take it easy!" as the officers roughly tried to handcuff her.

"Listen, man, I know you're a cop; but this lady is fighting like a crazed animal. Let us do our job. We're trying our best not to hurt her but you're not helping us by staying here."

Suddenly Joyce started snarling obscenities, and, as the officers literally carried her to the squad car, she spat at Nick. After she was secured in the backseat, Nick watched in horror as they exited the condo parking lot with the sirens blaring and lights flashing.

While the Public Information Officer from Hollywood Bay Police Department was fending off questions from the media, Nick observed Sheriff Wagner, Chief Fox, and Chief Thomas huddled in a tight circle. Deciding not to approach, he began to think about his twins.

"How do I tell my kids that their mother has been arrested for murder? How do I tell Joyce's parents about what has just taken place? God, I must have worked on at least twenty homicide cases in my career, but who would ever think the murderer would be someone you know? Especially not the mother of your children."

Seeing Tina standing off to the side he immediately made his way over to her. Wearing a blanket around her shoulders, she was shivering violently under it. As he put his arms around her, he hugged her saying, "Thank God, you're alright! This is all entirely my fault! I never should have let you get involved in this mess. I had no idea that Joyce was so sick. Tina, what can I do to make this up to you?"

Tina, trying to be supportive said, "Nick, don't worry about me. I'm kinda shook up now, but I'm going to be okay. You need to get home and be with your kids before they hear all kinds of rumors about you and Joyce." She then added, "I'm not going back to my apartment today. I'll be staying with friends for a few days." Kissing him on the cheek, she told him that she'd talk to him later and started to walk away.

Nick didn't see Tina's eyes fill with tears. They were tears of frustration and resignation. Deep down, Tina recognized that her relationship with Nick was over. He had his children who were going to need a full-time dad, and she, knowing herself, had to admit that she was not prepared to handle ten year old twins. Especially ones with so much baggage. "Who knows," she thought, "when they grow up and fully understand what's happened, they may blame me for their mother's breakdown."

Nick feeling totally dejected, thought, "Just when I'm sure things can't get much worse, they do. Here I am standing in the parking lot watching Tina walk out of my life knowing that there is nothing I can do to stop her."

Forced to deal with questions that still need answers, Nick approached the Chiefs, Sheriff and Manny Lopez. He asked Chief Fox where they had taken Joyce. Fox told him, "Memorial Healthcare on Johnson Street. They have an excellent psychiatric facility, and they will take good care of her. Everyone we Baker Act is sent there for evaluation."

Seeing the grief on his face Chief Thomas advised him that when Joyce got there she would be medicated. The admitting process and her evaluations would take all of the rest of the day and probably most of the day after. "Since you aren't going to be able to see her, may I suggest that you leave now and begin your drive home? If anything changes I promise one of us will call you. If I were you, I'd call my in-laws immediately and tell them what has happened before the press gets to them. Tell them to take the kids out of the house and not to turn on the TV. It's going to be all over the news if it isn't already.

Nick, if you have family or friends out of the area, now would be a good time for a visit. The news coverage is going to be national. If you think the local reporters are jackals, wait till you meet the real pros. Some of those guys would sell out their mothers for an exclusive with you and the twins."

Agreeing with the Chief, Nick accepted a ride back to the station from Manny. They drove in silence as neither one of them knew what to say.

Pulling up to the station, Manny stopped beside Nick's car and said, "Don't worry about the Durango. As soon as our guys are through with it, I'll make arrangements to have it driven to your home." Nick thanked him for his help and Manny nervously whispered, "Hey man, I'm really sorry for the way this all turned out."

Nick got into his car. As he headed for Alligator Alley, Nick picked up his phone and dialed his in-laws. Hoping that one of the twins wouldn't answer, he was relieved when he heard Eric's voice answer his call.

"Eric, this is Nick. Look, I've got something I need to share with both you and Toby. Can you get her to pick up the extension without letting the twins know I'm on the line?"

Hearing the tension in Nick's voice he called out, "Toby, pick up the phone."

Toby asked, "Who is it?"

He heard Eric say, "Just pick up the damn phone and stop asking so many questions."

Reaching for the phone she asked, "What is wrong with you? Who's on the line?" Before she can say anything else Nick said "Toby, it's me and don't let the kids know who you're talking to. Are the twins in the room with you?"

"No, I'm in the bedroom and the twins are in the den. Will you just tell me what the hell is going on?"

"Listen carefully, and please try not to react to what I'm going to tell you. Joyce has been arrested by the Sunset Beach Police Department and is being charged with four counts of murder." Before he can utter another word he heard a gut wrenching scream and a phone hitting the floor.

Hearing scrambling in the background he heard the twins yelling, "Poppie, Grams is sick!"

Rushing in from the kitchen, Eric picked up the phone in the bedroom before the twins had a chance and while comforting them tells them that Grams is alright. Smiling he said, "Grams just hit her funny bone on the table and you know what? It wasn't funny. So why don't you go back to the den to finish your homework. And don't forget to shut off the TV."

Waiting for them to leave the room, Eric then asked "What do you want me to do?"

Thinking for a moment Nick said, "Can you get the twins out of the house immediately? In the next few hours the media will be all over this. It will be on every TV station and in every newspaper. I'm on Alligator Alley and can be in Sanibel in less than two hours. Take the kids anywhere where they don't have access to a TV and I'll meet you at the Fresh Fruit Farm and Souvenir stand right off the Alley. It's the one that you always take the twins. Ask Toby if she could please throw some clothes in a bag for the twins. I'll make a reservation at a motel at least for tonight or until I can figure out what else to do. Eric, you need to do this quickly before all hell breaks loose."

Although he is in a total state of shock Eric said, "We'll meet you in the parking lot. Drive carefully."

Pulling off on to the side of the road, Nick tried to stop the shaking. Trying to come up with some kind of a plan, he called a motel right outside of Sanibel and after making a reservation pulled back on to the Alley. His thoughts went right back to the twins and he wondered how he was going to explain what has happened to their mom when he can't understand it himself. How can he convince them that she is not a monster, but someone who is sick and went out of control? He needs to figure out how to shield them from ignorant adults and cruel children who will now become a part of their lives. Feeling that the task is monumental, he allowed the tears that had been welling up to fall.

As Nick turns into the Fresh Fruit Farm and Souvenirs stand parking lot he recognized Eric's van and parked right behind it. Getting out of his car he saw Clyde still wearing his cumbersome cast, standing unsteadily behind Bonnie. Seeing Nick, Clyde asked, "What's going on, Dad?"

Looking at the twins, Nick can't help but notice the bewildered and frightened look on their faces. He reached out and hugged and kissed them both.

As the door to the van opened, Nick could see that Toby and Eric had been crying. Nick suddenly became aware that neither of the twins had asked about their mother. It was almost as if they knew something terrible had happened and were avoiding the subject.

Trying not to frighten them any more than they already were, Nick handed them each ten dollars and told them to order their favorite slushy drinks and also a snack. He hoped that this will give him the time he needed to tell his in-laws what had happened.

With the twins heading for the picnic area, Nick stepped into the van. He decided to be direct. "Let me tell you what I know and then we can figure out a way to help Joyce, if possible. This time she stepped over the line. She's in very serious trouble." Taking a deep breath Nick told them that that morning Joyce was arrested while attempting to murder the Medical Examiner from Broward County.

Skipping the details about his relationship with her, Nick continued. "Unfortunately, that's not the worst of it. She is also accused of murdering four women. Two here in Lee County and two others in Broward County. Remember the cases I was working on that were dubbed *The Golden Girls Murders*? Well, there is enough evidence to not only charge Joyce in these homicides but to convict her as well."

Toby beginning to sob exclaimed, "This is entirely my fault! I should have seen how sick she really was. Especially after the incident with Clyde."

Nick baffled asked, "What incident with Clyde?" What's been going on? For God's sake, Eric, what the hell is she talking about?"

Before Eric had a chance to answer, Nick saw the twins heading back toward the van. Enraged he turns to his in-laws and said, "Trust me, this conversation is not over. It will just have to wait until the twins are asleep."

Opening the door to the van, Bonnie stuck her head in and asked, "Why is everyone looking so mad at each other? Did we do something wrong?"

"Of course not, Darling," Nick said. "We were just having an adult conversation. Tell you what. You and Clyde hop in the van because we're going to stay at a motel tonight."

Clyde asked, "Why can't we ride with you?"

Answering him Nick said, "You know it's easier for you to sit in the van because there's more room for your cast, and besides, I have to pick some things up at Wal-Mart so I'll meet you there."

Arriving at the motel about ten minutes behind his in-laws, Nick found their van and parked next to it. Taking the packages from the trunk Nick heard the TV blasting from their room. As he opened the motel room door he was greeted by Bonnie saying, "Look, Daddy, you and Mommy are on TV!"

Looking at his in-laws in total disgust, he saw the screen filled with a close-up of Joyce. Her eyes are moving wildly like a trapped animal with no way out. As the cameras pulled back, the screen now showed Joyce struggling with two officers as they carried her to the waiting police car. Nick heard the reporter's voice saying, "Joyce Russo, seen here, is being taken into police custody and charged with four counts of first degree murder and one count of attempted murder. She is the wife of Detective Nick Russo from Lee County Sheriff's Department, a fifteen year veteran of the department.

Joyce Russo is thirty-five years old and the mother of twins. She is seen being transported to the psychiatric facility of Memorial Healthcare for evaluation.

Her husband, Detective Nick Russo, was on the scene but would not comment on the arrest of his wife."

Closing the segment with a picture of Nick and Joyce, the reporter concluded, "Stay turned for further details beginning at six."

Shutting off the TV, Nick was crushed by the look of horror in the twin's eyes. He told them to sit down on the bed beside him.

Ignoring Toby, who was standing near the door and crying, Nick told the twins that they were not responsible for anything that was happening to their mom. He explained that their mom was sick. He also said that no one knew yet if what the police said about her was true.

Clyde asked, "What did they say mom did?"

"Well, Son, they are saying that mom hurt some ladies very badly, but, if she did, I'm sure she didn't mean it."

Clyde rendered Nick speechless when he said, "I believe she did it. I bet she hurt those ladies just like she hurts Bonnie and me. I hope they keep her in jail. I wish she was the one that died!" Clyde screamed while the tears ran down his face.

Completely losing himself, he turned to Eric and Toby screaming "That's it! You're going to tell me what is going on or I'm going to throw you both out right now!"

Before they can answer, Nick looked at the twins and getting control of his temper, asked in a soft caring voice, "Was Mommy hitting you?"

Bonnie whispered, "Yes."

With a look of shock on his face, Nick said, "Why didn't you tell Grams or Poppie?"

Still angry Clyde said, "We did! When we would call, Poppie would pick us up and take us to his house for a few days until, like he said, Mommy would calm down."

"Why didn't you guys tell me?"

Bonnie said, "We couldn't because Mommy said she would really beat us if we said anything and we were afraid."

Clyde continued, "Remember when I was in the hospital? I tried to tell you about it. Bonnie told me that she was playing dress-up with Mommy's scarves, handbags and shoes. When mommy saw her, she hit her so hard that she banged her head on the closet door and cried. I remember that when I started to tell you about it mommy walked into the room and I got frightened again. After you left I told Bonnie to tell Grams. Bonnie said that Mommy told her that Grams used to hit her when she was little and would touch her things and she wouldn't care if mommy hit her *cause that's the way it was."*

Nick held the twins close and glared at his mother in-law. He was not prepared to hear what Clyde said next.

Looking straight at Nick, Clyde said, "I know Mommy told you I broke my leg playing with the kids in the backyard, but I didn't fall. Mommy pushed me down the steps 'cause I wasn't moving fast enough and she wanted to get by. She said I was doing it on purpose because she was late for an appointment, but I swear I wasn't. After I fell she told me to get up and go to my room. I told her that it hurt too much, and she said that I'd better be in my room when she got home. She just left me on the floor and slammed the door. Bonnie called Poppie and he came over and took me to the hospital. I had to wait a long time for the surgery because they couldn't find Mommy and Grams wouldn't call you." Stopping to catch his breath, Clyde wiped the tears from his eyes and said, "*I hope she never comes home. I hate her!*"

Turning to the twins Nick explained to them that he would never leave them alone again. "No matter what happens, the three of us will get through this together. I'm going to call your Aunt Sheila in Boca, and we're going to stay with her for a couple of days."

Turning to his in-laws and proud of his controlled voice, Nick said, "You both had better leave now before I say or do something stupid."

Facing Bonnie and Clyde, Nick in a spiteful tone said, "Children say good-bye to your grandparents."

Epilogue

Joyce Russo was committed to the State Hospital for the Criminally Insane in Chattahoochee, Florida, for an undetermined amount of time.

Tina Lange continued to work at the Medical Examiner's Office in Broward County.

Francine Bolton was permanently assigned to the FBI headquarters in Quantico, Virginia.

Nick Russo and his twins left Lee County and relocated to Palm Beach County to be closer to his sister.

Toby and Eric Stuart are living in the Orlando area so that they can visit their daughter Joyce when permitted.

Mac Thomas is still the Chief of Police of the Sunset Beach Police Department where he regularly meets with "The Ladies That Lunch."

About the Author

Marcia Slow-Sandler was raised in Brooklyn, New York. and relocated to Pembroke Pines Florida, with her husband Herb and their two sons Howard and Eric, in 1986.

Inspired by Angela Lansbury's T.V. portrayal of Jessica Fletcher, the crime solving author, Marcia decided to follow her footsteps "in real life." After her husband died, Marcia's hobby of mystery writing began in earnest.

To bring her characters to life and to add authenticity to her plots, Marcia draws from a wealth of personal experience acquired from her years of both serving Pembrome Pines and Hallandale Beach Police Departments as Crime Watch Coordinator and Public Information Officer.

She has received numerous awards throughout her career. In 2009, she was inducted into the Broward County Hall of Fame.

Still actively working, she is surrounded by her loving children and the "Sunshine of her LIfe" her granddaughter Nicole.

Printed in the United States
153555LV00004B/5/P